Something Pumping

By

Marie Rochelle

This is a work of fiction. Names, characters, places, and incidents are products of the author's imagination or are used fictitiously and are not to be construed as real. Any resemblance to actual events, locales, organizations, or persons, living or dead, is entirely coincidental.

Something Pumping by Marie Rochelle

Red Rose™ Publishing
Publishing with a touch of Class! ™
The symbol of the Red Rose and Red Rose is a trademark of Red Rose™ Publishing

Red Rose™ Publishing
Copyright© 2009 Marie Rochelle
ISBN: 978-1-60435-869-8
ISBN: 1-60435-869-6
Cover Artist: Shirley Burnett
Editor: Marguerite L. Lemons
Line Editor: WRFG

Red Rose™ Publishing
www.redrosepublishing.com
Forestport, NY 13338

Thank you for purchasing a book from Red Rose™Publishing where publishing comes with a touch of Class!

Chapter One

Driving down the long stretch of the road with the wind blowing through her curls, Jaleena Falcon tried to swallow her bitter disappointment at finding nothing to meet her needs at the flea markets. She had gotten up two hours early for *nothing*. She was searching for some extra pieces of furniture for her store. Yet, her latest hunt turned up zilch and she wasn't happy about going back empty handed. It always gave her such pleasure to buy older pieces no one else wanted and then turn them into treasures for someone else.

Jaleena turned the corner and was headed towards her shop when something at the side of the deserted highway made her lean across her steering wheel. She couldn't believe what she was seeing. There was no way that she could be this lucky. Sure, she was good at finding things but after her horrible morning. She had given up all hope about discovering a diamond in the rough. However, it seemed like things were improving for her after all, and she couldn't be happier. Not twenty feet in front of her was a gorgeous black loveseat that someone had tossed away.

In the past, Jaleena had been fortunate enough to find abandoned pieces here before, but never anything like this. She drove pass the loveseat a little bit, turned off her truck and got out. If everything turned out the way Jaleena hoped, she had just found the star piece for her grand opening tomorrow. People didn't understand how shabby chic was such a profitable business nowadays.

Bending down, she felt her skinny jeans stretch across her ass and in the back of her mind; she could hear her mother saying. *Jaleena, girl you know better than to wear pants that tight. You need some breathing room.* She quickly shoved the memory of her wonderful mother away before she started to cry.

Reaching out, she checked the sofa more closely and didn't see a thing wrong with it. *What was wrong with whoever pitched this out?* She was astonished someone would just toss away expensive furniture for no apparent reason. However, what was that old saying '*someone else's junk is another person's treasure*'? Well, she had found a gem with this couch and she wasn't about to leave it here. This would bring in an excellent price at her consignment store '*Nothing Too Old.*'

Dashing back to her truck, Jaleena backed it up until the lift she had installed on it was in front of the couch.

Working the controls inside her vehicle, she got the couch moved and placed in the back without any problems.

Jaleena glanced in the rearview mirror to make sure there weren't any cars coming and pulled back out on the street. As she drove back towards her place of business, she remembered what made her want to start *Nothing Too Old* in the first place—her wonderful mother.

Her dreams of owning her own business came about when she was a little girl and her mother would wake her up early for their weekly Saturday visits to rummage sales. It was the favorite part of her week during the summer time. The week couldn't go by fast enough for her back then. Like clockwork at seven o'clock on Saturday morning her mother would holler upstairs at her. "Jaleena, child you better be up and dressed if you want to go with me."

What her mother didn't realize was she was already dressed and about to race down the stairs. She loved riding her pink Huffy bicycle back then and it would already be outside waiting for her without her even asking for it.

Laughing to herself, Jaleena ran her fingers through her hair and recalled how she loved learning the ropes of being a good second-hand shopper. Back then, she studied very closely how her mama would check objects to see how good or bad a condition they were in.

She also learned something else as a child by watching the ladies with the huge diamonds rings on their fingers. She saw how they would try to cheat the person having the yard sale out of their money by asking for lower prices. She wasn't dumb as a little girl. She could tell they had the money to buy it, but wanted to see if they could trick the seller into selling for next to nothing. However, most of the time the person having the yard sale would tell them no and the person would leave pissed off.

In addition, one of her other favorite yard sale memories was when one lady had Golden Retriever puppies and she played with one of them in her backyard. Since the apartments where she lived with her family didn't allow pets that had made her entire day.

"Mama, I miss you so much," Jaleena sighed inside the truck as she finished reminiscing about her past. She had been best friends with her mother and it had devastated her beyond belief when her mother passed away. Yet, she knew her mother was smiling down from heaven, because her baby girl has made her dreams of owning her own business finally come. "I'm going to continue to make you proud of me," Jaleena swore to herself. *Nothing Too Old*, was as much her dream as her mother's and she wasn't about to let it fail for the either of them.

Chapter Two

Cage Harrison had just finished zipping up his pants and was looking for a shirt in his closet when two soft hands wrapped around his waist. He didn't even have to guess who it was.

"Katlyn, how many times have I told you to knock before you come inside my house?"

"Baby, I did knock but you must have been in the shower and didn't hear me," Katlyn whined running her hands up and down his chest. "I have missed you and I came by to see if you wanted to have dinner with me tonight."

Grabbing a gray sleeveless T-shirt out of the closet, Cage brushed Katlyn's hands off his body and stepped away from her. He had been dating Katlyn McGillis on and off for a few months now, but it wasn't anything serious on his part. Yet, she couldn't seem to understand that.

Sure, the sex had been great at first, but now he was looking for something more. All Katlyn wanted him to do was stay in her bedroom twenty four hours a day, seven days a week. He wasn't the type of man to be kept by any woman. He had a job and he loved working. However, Katlyn acted like she never believed the words coming out of his mouth and he was tired of repeating himself when it came to her.

He should have listened to River when he had the chance too and now he was caught up in a situation he couldn't get out of. His godfather warned him about getting involved with an older woman because Katlyn might become possessive of him and their time together.

However, back then he didn't think the six year age difference would matter that much. He was thirty-four and Katlyn was only forty. He made the bad mistake of thinking both of them had gone into this relationship with their eyes wide open, but now he was seeing how wrong he was. Katlyn didn't want to leave him alone. She wanted to be in his life *forever* and wasn't about to let him leave her for any reason. He was running out of ways to tell her in a nice way that they weren't a couple anymore.

It wasn't like Katlyn wasn't a stunning woman with her flame red hair, dark green eyes and tall, athletic model body. He had mentioned to her a couple of times that she couldn't get any skinner. But his comments went in one ear and right out of the other, so he just stopped saying it.

Katlyn thought the skinner she was the prettier she was. Honestly, in his opinion, she could have any man she set her sights on, yet it seemed like she was hooked only on him.

"Hey, there's no need to get dressed now that I'm here," Katlyn took the shirt from him and tossed it on the bed. She reached for his zipper and started pulling it down. "I missed you so much. I'm so glad that I caught you at home." She tried kissing him on the mouth, but he quickly turned his head so it landed on his cheek instead.

He didn't want to hurt Katlyn feelings, but he truly wasn't interested in a sexual relationship with her anymore. She became a little too clingy for him. He liked his women into him; however Katlyn had just gone over board with her constant affections. It almost came across now as neediness on her part. Hell, it was almost borderline obsession and he couldn't let it go any further. He was going to have to have another talk with her.

"Katlyn, haven't I told you time and time again it's over between us? You can't keep doing this." Placing his hands on her shoulders, Cage gently moved Katlyn away from him. He quickly zipped his pants grabbed his shirt off the bed and put it on.

"I'm hungry and was about to grab something to eat. Do you want to come with me? I think we really need to talk about us again," he asked.

It was now or never. He had to get Katlyn to understand that they weren't a couple anymore. Sadly, a part of him thought they could at least be friends, but he was seeing now that wasn't even a possibility. He was trying his best to make the spilt between them a pleasant experience. So they could both walk away without having any bad feelings for the other person.

Katlyn glared at him like she was going to say something else, but ended up changing her mind. "Fine, I'll go to lunch with you because I've missed you. However, I do not believe you when you tell me that things are over."

Cage decided not to get into an argument about this inside his house. A place full of people would be better to finally make Katlyn understand that he meant business about them being over. Grabbing Katlyn's hand, he led her from his bedroom, "Come on I'll take you to that Chinese restaurant you love so much."

"Whew!" Jaleena sighed as she made it into the coolness of her shop and out of the hot sun. She never thought that she was going to make it back here in time. Sometimes it seemed like the drive from her bargain hunting trips to *Nothing Too Old* took forever, but in reality it was about the same time every day.

"Tyrell...Tyrell...where are you?"

She knew her brother was here somewhere, because she called him and told him to open the place early with the spare key she gave him. *So, where in the hell was he?* It took about five minutes before her brother came from the back of her shop with a large sandwich in his hand.

"Hell Sis, you don't have to scream like that. I'm not deaf," Tyrell complained.

"Tyrell, I don't have time for your attitude today," she snapped back. "I need you to help me with the piece of furniture I was lucky enough to find."

"WHAT?" Tyrell uttered with the sandwich halfway to his mouth. "Why do I always have to help you? What kind of junk have you dragged here now? Why can't you buy it new and then resell it? You got half of mother's money from her estate when she died. You don't have to put raggedy ass crap in here all the damn time. You try calling it shabby chic, but it's a place full of cast-offs and we both know it. I thought you would be smarter than to invest in this rat hole of a place."

The nerve of him!

How dare her lazy ass brother think he can talk to her like that! It's not like he had done something with his life. The last time she checked he was still looking for a job.

She was getting so tired of Tyrell and his "pissy" attitude. "Shut up, Tyrell. Just shut the hell up. Mother left us the money without any stipulations. She knew how each one of us would use it."

"You're just pissed because you're broke. It isn't my fault you wasted your half trying to impress your friends. I bought this little shop and redecorated it the way I wanted to. Why didn't you make a better investment with your half?"

"There you go with that blame shit," Tyrell shouted at her. "You were always mama's favorite anyway, because you went to those stupid yard sales with her. I never got to go to them. You were the one she always took with her and did things with. You were constantly getting special treatment while I was left abandoned."

Jaleena couldn't believe Tyrell was trying to pull this shit with her. "You know mama tried taking you with us.

The couple of times that she did you stole things. Stealing at a garage sale was ridiculous and that's why mama started leaving you at home.

"She didn't want to have to look over her shoulder the entire time when you came with us. She shouldn't have had to worry about keeping an eye on you and preventing your five finger discounts. It was wrong for you to even put her in that position in the first place."

"I wasn't really stealing," Tyrell complained, waving the sandwich in front of her face. "Hell, it was a yard sale. It was mostly useless items that I stole anyway. It wasn't like they were going to miss any of that crap. All of these second-hand goods in here remind me of the places that mama used to take you. I thought the stuff you came back home with was worthless back then and it still is now."

That was it!

She wasn't going to deal with her ungrateful brother anymore. She could find someone else to help here get the couch out of the back of the truck. Tyrell wouldn't do anything but complain the whole time anyway.

"Get out! Get out now!" Jaleena screamed at her brother. "I thought letting you come here after you get out of prison would be a good thing. I hoped that you had changed, but I was so wrong. You're still no good and want to cause trouble any chance you get." "Stop acting so melodramatic," Tyrell sighed, rolling his eyes at her. "Shouldn't you have outgrown all of that by now? You're a grown woman get your shit together and act like one."

Anger swept through Jaleena's body as her brother insulted her. Why in the hell was he telling her to get her shit together when half the time he didn't have a clue what was going on in his own damn head. Wasn't he the one who got sent away to prison instead of cutting a deal like his so-called friends did? They turned on him at the drop of a hat.

"Tyrell, you need to watch what you say to me, because you know that eventually you'll be begging for my help like you always do. Next time, I might leave you ass out to dry."

Her brother moved closer in a menacing manner until his chest almost was touching hers. "You aren't going to do anything of the sort, little sister."

"You don't know how not to help me. You're just like our silly mother. She always threatened not to get me out of trouble, but ended up doing it every time I came to her.

You're cut from the same cloth. So, learn to deal with it." Tyrell smirked at her before taking a huge bite out of the sandwich in his hand.

Jaleena felt her blood racing through her veins as Tyrell insulted the memory of their loving mother. She fought the urge to slap the taste out of his mouth. Taking a deep breath, she tried to calm herself down. She didn't want to end up getting arrested for kicking her brother's skinny ass.

"I know that you probably didn't leave me any food in the refrigerator for my opening. So, why don't you take what you have in your hand and get the hell out of my sight before I do something I might regret later."

"Oh, by the way, I hope you enjoy every damn bite because believe this. It will be the last fucking thing you will get from me. Now, get your thieving ass out of my store."

Tyrell's eyes swung down to the sandwich in his hand and then he tossed her a hateful look. "Take this damn sandwich. I don't need it," he snapped throwing it in her direction.

Jaleena jumped back just before the food hit her in the chest. *Oh, no he just didn't throw that food at her!*

She had this place clean and her brother wasn't going to mess it up. "Stop acting like a bastard," she yelled. "You better pick that sandwich up and toss it in the trash.

Her brother narrowed his hazel eyes at her as a dark look came over his face. "Fine, I'll clean it up, but you won't like where I stick it this time." Reaching down, Tyrell snatched up the sandwich, spun around on his heel and rushed in the direction of the bathroom. Seconds later, she heard a loud splash and then her brother yelled out from the other room at her. "There I got rid of it. Are you happy now?"

Jaleena stood in shock as she heard the toilet flush and then raced into the bathroom. She got there just in time to see the thick sandwich trying to go down, but it kept floating around in the toilet and she knew it was stopped up.

"Look at what you did," Jaleena hollered hitting her brother in the shoulder. Reaching inside the toilet, she grabbed the soggy remains of the sandwich and threw it at Tyrell. "I can't believe you just did this shit to me. Your ass better hand me that plunger at the side of the toilet and you better pray I can I get this crap out of there."

Tyrell wiped the food off his clothing. "If you weren't my sister, I would knock the hell out of you for throwing food from the toilet on me. However, I know you would call the cops on me and have me back in jail."

Shoving past her, Tyrell tossed her a dirty look. "I don't see a plunger. So, I guess you're out of luck little sister," he snickered as he left her alone in the bathroom.

"I don't believe you." Jaleena went over to the other side of the toilet and searched for the plunger, but it was nowhere in sight. It had to be there. She just got a new one yesterday and placed it right here. Where did it go? "Tyrell, I know you did something with that plunger. Why are you purposely trying to ruin the most important day of my life? Just because you ruined your dreams by going down the wrong road"

"I'll be damned if I stand by and let you destroy mine. Give me back the plunger and get out like I have been telling you." She hollered following her brother back into the front of the store. "I'm not going to waste the rest of my day dealing with your antics."

"I didn't touch that thing. What in the hell would I need with it? Maybe it's stuck in your ass and that's why you're such a bitch to me all of the time."

Jaleena wasn't going to get into another argument with Tyrell. He was constantly finding a way to push her buttons and today she didn't have time for it. Since she knew he was lying to her and would keep lying she had to find a plumber and see if he would be able to fix her problem. She remembered cutting an ad out of the newspaper the other day.

Going around Tyrell, she made her way to her office located in the very back of *Nothing Too Old*. Jaleena made her way over to her desk and stared at the pile of papers on it.

"I know I tossed that newspaper clipping here yesterday. I hope I can find it and they can help me. If I can't tomorrow is going to be ruined for me." She searched through the sheets of paper until she found the ad.

"Thank God," Jaleena sighed as she picked up the clipping and read it out loud:

Something Pumping
24 Hour Plumbing Service
If you need us we can be found
Reasonable Rates
Call (265) 691-0000

"I hope this ad is the real deal," Jaleena prayed to herself as she grabbed the phone and dialed the phone number. It rang at least four times, and she was about to hang up when a male voice finally answered the phone.

"24 hour plumbing, River speaking, how many I help you?" he asked in a professional manner.

Jaleena almost jumped for joy at getting a live voice and not a tape recording. "Yes, I'm calling about your ad. Do you think you can come out and help me? I have a serious problem with my toilet. I mean it's really bad."

"What kind of problem, Miss," the man inquired on the other end of the phone?

"It's my toilet. Food has been flushed down it and now it's stopped up. It was flushed a couple of times and now the water is starting to overflow."

"Did you try using a plunger? Maybe that will get it out for you?" He suggested. "I want to get a feel for what you have already done before I send someone out there."

"I don't have a plunger, so I'm in desperate need of help. Can you please send someone out here to help me?" Jaleena knew she was practically begging for help and she didn't give a damn.

"I think I can get someone out there to see you, but I'm not positive."

"Sir, I'm having an open house tomorrow for my new business. Please try to find someone. I really need this bathroom fixed. Your ad does say you are open 24 hours. Can't you find anyone to come here and fix my problem?" Jaleena glanced over her shoulder as Tyrell strolled into her office looking smug. She didn't have time to deal with his crazy ass right now.

"Miss, calm down," the guy said softly trying to soothe her nerves. . "Yes, I can send someone over there today. Give me your address and I'll get him to you ASAP."

"My address is: 521 Alcoa Street. It's a small furniture store on the left hand side. It's called, *Nothing Too Old*."

"Okay, hang tight. I should have him there in an hour maybe less. I know it's a Saturday evening, but someone will be there."

"Wonderful, I'll be here." Jaleena told the guy before she hung up.

"I can't believe you're throwing such a fit over that stupid toilet," Tyrell complained glaring at her.

"Listen, I don't have time for your nonsense. You better hope this guy can fix my toilet or you're going to be in a lot of trouble with me." Jaleena threatened her eyes narrowing at her brother.

Tyrell dashed across the room and got directly in her face. The cold look in his eyes sent a chill down her spine. "Jaleena, you're my sister, but I'm getting tired of your threats. So, you better stop it now or you won't like the outcome at all."

Jaleena swallowed hard trying to think of a way to get Tyrell out of her shop, but nothing was coming to mind. She shouldn't be terrified of her brother, yet she was. The time he spent in prison had changed him and it wasn't for the better.

Chapter Three

"You know that I loathe going to the movies, but you always take me to those things," Katlyn grumbled staring at him across the table. He had to leave the movie early because of her continuous whining.

"Katlyn, you know that I enjoy going to the movies when I have free time away from my job. Why do you constantly act like you don't know that?" Cage asked glancing at his watch, trying to think of away to get rid of Katlyn.

"Besides I told you I wanted to see that movie before I had something to eat, you didn't have to tag along with me, but you did. Don't blame me if you had a bad time. It was your fault, not mine. Didn't I leave early? That should make you feel good. Now, I have to go back later by myself to see how it ends."

"You do remember that I want you to be my date for the Mayor's Ball next month to benefit those disadvantaged children that I help," Katlyn continued like he hadn't even spoken a word. "I already have the perfect suit picked out for you. You're going to love it. It will look amazing on your body."

Cage could barely hold his temper in check as he glared across the table at Katlyn. This wasn't working out between them, but she seemed to have a hard time understanding what he was telling her.

"No, Katlyn. I have told you to stop trying to put me in situations with your friends. It's not me and I don't like being around them. Can't you comprehend that we aren't together anymore? What else can I do to make you realize that?"

"Well, Mayor Greenwell's money wasn't too horrific for you to take last week when you fixed his sink. So, what is the big deal about being my date for this dinner party? Everyone knows that we're a couple," Katlyn said. "Why are you trying to deny what we feel for each other? I don't care about the age difference. You shouldn't feel embarrassed by it either. The whole town thinks we are practically living together."

"I don't care what the whole town thinks. This is the last time we're going to be seen out together. We have both outgrown each other and it's about time you grasp that. We need to go out separate ways." Cage prayed that

Katlyn finally dropped her fantasy about them being together forever because he didn't know if he could be any nicer to her.

Katlyn gave him a strange look and he could tell from the expression on her face that she was about to say something. However, his cell phone started ringing and thankfully cut off whatever she was going to tell him. Cage silently praised the person on the other end before he answered it.

"Cage speaking," he said into the phone.

"Cage, I hate to bother you on your date," River said.

"River, what is it?" He hoped it was something that would take him away from Katlyn. The situation was getting out of hand so fast.

"We got a call at 521 Alcoa Street. I think it's about a forty-five minute ride from where you're at. A woman called about a problem with her toilet. Do you think you can go and take a look at it for me? I would go myself but you're closer."

Cage looked at Katlyn and saw the determined look in her eyes. She wasn't about to give him a break about the Mayor's party. He had to get out of here before he said something that he wouldn't be able to take back. One thing he couldn't stand was a *needy* woman—when it came to that one word, Katlyn was at the top of the list.

"That's not a problem. I'll leave right now and check it out. I have all the equipment I need in the truck. Thanks for the phone call, River." Disconnecting the phone call, Cage shoved the phone back into the pocket of his jeans. This wasn't going to go well, but he had to get out of here and Katlyn was going to be pissed at him.

"That was River on the phone there's a plumbing problem I need to take care of. So, I need to leave." Cage stood up hoping to make a fast exit without Katlyn giving him any problems.

"Okay...I hope you can get it fixed, but don't forget to give me a call later." She looked at him like she really wanted to argue with him, but at the last minute changed her mind.

"Sure," Cage responded and then rushed out of the building. He wasn't about to call her about anything ever again.

Chapter Four

Jaleena was getting fed up with Tyrell's nasty ass attitude. She didn't know why he was still here. He wasn't helping her at all. The only thing he knew how to do well was make her life more difficult.

"Tyrell, I think you should leave. You have done enough destruction for one day. Honestly, I'm not sure if I even want to see your face again in my store." Her mother raised her to love her brother, but this was the final straw. Tyrell wasn't going to ruin her dream for her because he decided to make bad decisions that would adversely affect his life. She couldn't allow his poison to spill over into her life.

Racing across the room, Tyrell yanked her roughly by her upper arm, and the force of the action throwing her off balance and causing her to bump his body. "I'm so fucking tired of you acting like you are so much better than me! Mama is dead, so you aren't the precious little princess anymore. You're just like anyone else and I don't have a problem telling your ass what I think."

"Stop it Tyrell! Let go of my arm." Jaleena tried wrestling her arm away, but Tyrell wouldn't let it go.

"Just shut the hell up!"

"What in the hell is wrong with you today? I know you can get in these moods, but today is the worse. Don't you know that you may have ruined my Grand Opening tomorrow?" She tried not to flinch as her brother's fingers dug into her arm.

"I need some money," Tyrell exclaimed.

"Money...why do you need that?" she questioned.

She should have known that he would be asking her for money because that was all he ever did now. Tyrell wouldn't know how to earn a paycheck if his soul depended on it. He was always trying to get money from someone and now the person was her.

"I need a thousand dollars. Give it to me and I'll let your sorry ass alone."

"A thousand dollars," Jaleena gasped stunned by the amount. "Have you lost your mind? You were given five thousand dollars from mama's will. What did you do with all of that? Did you waste it on drugs or cheap women?"

Anger flashed in Tyrell's light brown eyes. He actually looked like he was about to strike her until he got himself under control. "I made some bad investments. That's all. Now be a good little sister and give me the money. I just need a thousand dollars. Damn it! I know you have it. You never spend anything. I'm really surprised you spent any money at all and on this dump."

Jaleena quickly swallowed the nasty retort as it worked its way up her throat. She didn't need to piss off her brother anymore than he already was. Tyrell had a bad temper and she wasn't ready to deal with it today. However, he wasn't going to bully her into giving him that money either. He made his bed and now he was going to have to lie in it-fleas and all.

"No!" She screamed trying to twist away from him again. "Get your hands off me and leave me the hell alone."

Cage knew that the two people fighting didn't see him standing there. He couldn't believe how the guy was manhandling the woman. He wasn't going to stand by and let him keep doing this to her. The guy had to be at least six feet compared to the woman's smaller height.

"Did you not hear what the lady said?" Cage demanded coming further into the room. He moved his work bag around on his shoulder as he tried to keep his cool.

The two people's heads spun around in his direction at the sound of his voice. Cage felt like he had gotten punched in the stomach when his eyes connected with the woman's. Her eyes were such a dark brown that they almost looked back. Long spiral curls brushed her milk chocolate shoulders. She looked at him and then back at the guy with the death grip on her arm.

For some reason he felt an intense urge to go over and kill that guy for putting his hands on her like that. She was trying to pretend that she wasn't in pain, but he could see the discomfort shining in her beautiful eyes.

"Who the fuck are you?" The guy yelled at him.

"I'm the plumber. I'm here to fix the toilet. I called out when I came in. However, I doubt either one of you could hear me above the screaming," Cage replied still glaring at the guy who had a death grip on the woman's arm.

"Do you mind letting her go now? I think you've gotten your point across."

"You can't tell me what in the hell to do. Who in the fuck do you think you are?"

Cage was trying to keep calm, but the guy was starting to piss him off. "I think you're hurting her. Don't you see the pain in her eyes?" He couldn't tear his gaze away from the woman's striking face. He had noticed black women before, but the woman in front of him was truly breathtaking.

"Did she tell you she was in pain?"

"Tyrell, let go of my arm," the softening of the woman's eyes made Cage's gut clench. It was like music to his ears.

"Jaleena, are you going to give me the money or not?" Tyrell asked releasing her arm.

"There's some money under the counter out front. It's in a metal box. That's all the money I have and after you take it I want you out of here, and I mean don't step a foot in my place again."

Cage watched how Jaleena rubbed the upper part of her arm and he suppressed the urge to hit Tyrell in his face. They were almost the same height, but he definitely had a muscle advantage on the younger man. He didn't know Jaleena, but the urge to protect her was strong and he was about to act on it if Tyrell touched her again.

"I'll take that, but I know it isn't going to be enough." Tyrell brushed past Jaleena and tossed him a threatening look before storming out of the room.

A second or two later the sound of the front door to the shop being slammed shut echoed through the building.

Cage was pleased Tyrell was finally gone or something was going to happen because of the way he was treating Jaleena.

"Sorry, you had to see that," Jaleena apologized. "But I'm glad you came in or my brother might have never left." She tried to give him a small smile to ease the tension in the room, but it didn't work.

The guy who was manhandling Jaleena was her own brother? What in the world was wrong with him? "Does he always treat you like that?" Cage didn't want to be nosy, but he couldn't tolerate a man who abused a woman. Jaleena might not have had a chance against Tyrell if he hadn't come in here.

"Tyrell hasn't had the best of luck and he feels like the world owes him. He doesn't like taking no for an answer."

"Isn't that going to make life even harder on him?" he questioned. "I mean there are a lot of people in this world. I'm sure some of them are going to tell him no more than once."

Jaleena's eyes sparkled as though she found his comment funny. "I think I'm going to like you a lot Mr...?"

Stepping forward, Cage extended his hand. "Cage Harrison," he said. "It's very nice to meet you."

"Jaleena Falcon. It's very nice to meet you too," Jaleena said shaking his hand and then letting it go sooner than he wanted. He loved how soft her skin was. "I hope that you can fix the problem with my toilet. I can't believe Tyrell did this to me. He knows how much tomorrow means to me. He's always trying to ruin stuff for other people."

"I haven't met a problem toilet that I couldn't' fix," Cage grinned, not knowing what it was doing to the woman in front of him.

Jaleena was trying her best not to notice how sexy, tall, and handsome Cage Harrison was. The gray sleeveless T-shirt stretched across his chest displaying toned, tanned bare arms to perfection and they were turning her on. She didn't know the last time she had been around a man *this* good-looking. God, his body was so fit. There wasn't a doubt in her mind that he worked out hard to keep his physique in tip top shape. She secretly wondered if Cage could work her out that well too?

His gray eyes bored into hers and she wondered what he was thinking. Did he find her as cute as she found him? Would he go out on a date with her if she asked? Taking a quick peek at his ring finger she noticed it was bare.

When she called for a plumber she never thought she would be getting someone that would look like this. He totally put all those other crack showing plumbers to shame. How could Cage be a plumber when his body was made for modeling? Okay, she needed to calm down so she wouldn't stumble over her words. Cage was hot enough to make any woman tongue tied.

"Okay...Ms. Falcon. Do you mind showing me where the toilet is so I can get it started?" Cage broke into her thoughts, making Jaleena wonder how long she had been standing there gawking at him.

God, she hoped there wasn't a line of drool coming out of the side of her mouth. She resisted the urge to wipe her hand across the side of her mouth. That would be too embarrassing if it came back damp.

"Jaleena will be fine," she corrected then spun around. "Follow me. The toilet is right this way." Making sure not to look over her shoulder, Jaleena took Cage towards the back of the store and the broken toilet.

Chapter Five

Sitting his work bag down on the floor, Cage stood over the toilet looking at the food floating around in it. He wondered what exactly was going on with her. Whatever it was there was a lot more to it than this stopped up toilet. Jaleena and her brother Tyrell had a violate relationship.

"Does your brother always treat you like that?" he asked looking at the pretty woman standing next to him. It had been such a long time since he had been around a woman who made him stop working just to stare at her.

Jaleena brushed a curl off her shoulder and avoided his direct stare. "Tyrell has a temper and sometimes it gets the best of him. However, I won't stand for him manhandling me like that. He better stay away from me or I'm going to call the police next time. His parole officer won't be happy if he gets into anymore trouble. Tyrell is already walking a thin line with him as it is. "

Cage wanted to say more, but he didn't feel like it was his place. He barely knew this woman and all he could think about was defending her. This has never happened to him before, and he wasn't sure how to handle it. Maybe it would be better if he stayed on the topic at hand, Jaleena's toilet problem.

"Do you know exactly what he flushed down there?" Cage asked. Bending down, he unzipped his bag and pulled out a plunger, drop cloth and a couple of rags. Placing the drop cloth and rags around the toilet he waited for Jaleena's answer.

"It was a large sandwich. Tyrell tossed it in there and flushed it before I could stop him," Jaleena said moving closer to him. "Do you think you can fix it? I can't have people here tomorrow and no toilet for them to use."

"I won't leave until I get this fixed." Taking the plunger, Cage used it a couple of times and more food came up, but he could tell that it was still stopped up. "Do you have a trash can?"

While Jaleena went to get him a trash can Cage grabbed a pair of rubber gloves and pulled them on. Jaleena came back in the room and placed the trash can next to his bag.

"Thanks," he said. Reaching down, he grabbed the food and tossed it into the trashcan. "I think there is something else down there besides the sandwich Tyrell forced in there."

"Damn him," Jaleena cursed behind him. "I can't believe he would do this to me. He knows how much time and not to mention money I put into tomorrow. I know he doesn't like the idea of *Nothing Too Old*, but I didn't think he would attempt to sabotage me like this."

"Tyrell doesn't seem like a very nice guy." Cage made the comment as he was pulling the snake out of his bag. "Now, if anything is in there this plumber's snake will find it for you."

Inserting the snake into the toilet, Cage gradually turned it as he inserted the spring into the drain. He kept moving it around until he felt something catch on the end of the hook. He slowly started to pull it out until the item came out of the stopped up toilet.

"Here's what started the problem." Grabbing the dirty washrag off the end, he showed it to Jaleena before he tossed it into the trash can.

"I can't believe him! Why in the hell did he do that? I swear if he shows his face here again I'm going to have him arrested. I'm not playing with him this time."

Cage started to clean up his stuff as he thought the same thing Jaleena did, but again he kept his comments to himself. It wasn't his place to tell Jaleena what she should do with her life. Tyrell was her brother and she might just be saying these things now because she was angry and then change her mind later.

Standing up, he faced Jaleena and he couldn't get over how stunning she truly was. There was just something about her that made him want to shield her. Despite the fact, she seemed quite capable of handling any situation that was tossed her way. He had been around black women before and had always found them very attractive. However, this is the first time he thought of asking one out on a date. From past experience, he knew there were some black women who still didn't date outside of their race.

Back in high school when he was on the football team, the black cheerleaders talked to him, but they always went out with the black players. Sure when he was younger, he wasn't the best looking guy in the world. Yet, he knew how to play football and that helped him get a spot on the team. He loved being a football player and benefited from the perks that went along with it.

However, his life changed after he decided to become a plumber. For some reason, he started working out more, drinking protein drinks and adding much needed muscle to his slim frame. Women noticed the difference in him. They were constantly asking him out. Slipping their phone numbers in his hands, pockets and anywhere they could place them. From the way they acted towards him, it was like he was an exotic male dancer at a bachelorette party or something.

Dragging himself away from reminiscing over his past, Cage looked down at Jaleena's lips and wondered how they would taste. What would she do if he kissed her right now? Did she sense the same attraction he did? Or was it all in his mind?

Chapter Six

"Cage, are you okay?" Jaleena asked touching him on the arm. She was having a hard time paying attention with Cage so close to her. The heat from his body was making her body burn and making her wonder about things she shouldn't.

I wonder if he's single, she thought.

After taking another quick look at him she shook that thought from her head and eased her hand away from his body. There was no way a man that damn HOT was single.

"I'm okay. I'm just pissed your brother did this to you. Why would he want to sabotage you?" Cage asked.

"With Tyrell, I never know what's going on with him or the way he thinks. He has been like that ever since we were young. Sometimes, I forget that he's the oldest because I'm always taking care of him," Jaleena complained. "But enough about my brother I want to thank you so much for fixing my problem. If you hadn't shown up I don't know what I would have done."

"I'm glad there was no really huge problem to fix," Cage smiled. "You just have a little water cleanup that missed the protective covering I put down. Everything should go smoothly for you tomorrow."

Jaleena felt like a weight had been lifted off her shoulders. "I'm so happy to hear that. It took me six months to find this place. I loved it from the first moment I stepped inside."

"I wish you the best of luck with your business. I remember how nervous I was when I decided to open up my plumbing business. It was a lot of hard work at first. I had to build up my clients, but it was worth all the sweat and tears." Reaching out, Cage touched her on the shoulder and a light shock traveled through her body.

Jaleena didn't break eye contact with Cage. She wanted to see if he felt the same sizzling rush that she did. The shocked look on his face quickly answered her unspoken question. It had been years since she had been this drawn to a man without knowing anything about him.

She had always been very level-headed when it came to the opposite sex. However, she couldn't ignore how her heart was racing and her palms were a little sweaty. Cage was standing so close to her and all sorts of wicked fantasizes were going through her mind.

Stop it now! She scolded herself.

Sure, she was pretty certain that Cage was attracted to her. But that didn't mean he wanted to ask her out on a date. Jaleena mentally told herself to move away from Cage before she humiliated herself and probably him too.

"Hmmm...would you like a tour of the place before you leave?" Jaleena asked.

"I would love one," Cage replied, removing his hand and she missed his touch immediately. "Let me clean this stuff up first."

"Great. I'll be in the front of the store waiting for you." Brushing past Cage, she tried not to moan as the side of her breast brushed against his tanned arm. Lord, it wasn't right for one man to possess so much virility.

Cage watched how well the jeans hugged Jaleena's ass as she moved pass him into the other room. He had never been jealous of a piece of clothing until now. Jaleena was hot as hell and he was trying to figure out a way to ask her out to dinner and maybe a movie afterwards. She was just the type of woman he had been looking for. Jaleena was so different from Katlyn and that was in a good way.

Jaleena was strong and independent. He'd already figured that much out from watching her deal with her threatening brother and his issues. Yet, he could also tell that she had a fun and outgoing personality. He loved those qualities in a woman.

In the beginning of his on again and off again relationship with Katelyn, she pretended to have those qualities and he had admired that about her. However, all of that changed when they started having sex, she quickly became jealous and controlling. If he even smiled at the waitress taking their order, she would think he was sleeping with her. That insecurity of hers got old quick and it was one of the main reasons he decided to end things between them.

It was a good thing he finally broke things off with Katlyn. He didn't want anything, or anyone standing in the way of him dating Jaleena, but he had to make sure she was interested in him first. He had a feeling that she was. Now, all he had to do was see if his intuition was right or wrong about what he sensed between them because he wasn't about to assume anything.

Getting a dry rag out of his bag of supplies on the floor, Cage cleaned off the snake and placed it back into bag along with everything else he had used to fix the toilet. He hurriedly cleaned up the little spots of water off the floor before tossing the rag in the trash can.

Washing his hands in the sink, Cage dried them on a towel while thinking of a way to approach Jaleena to see if she wanted to spend some time with him. He couldn't waste anymore time in the bathroom. Jaleena was waiting to show him around her business and after they were finished he would just suggest they go out to dinner. The worst thing she could tell him was no.

"Don't come on to strong. Flirt with her a little. Compliment her and then dive in to the good stuff. Ask her out." Cage kept coaching himself as he picked up his bag and headed out the bathroom door.

God, I hope she doesn't turn me down.

Chapter Seven

Moving through her store, Jaleena pointed out her favorite pieces to Cage while trying to block out how good he smelled walking next to her. She always had a thing for blue collar men and Cage most definitely fit the image she loved so much. It was such a shame nothing would ever come out of her attraction to him. There was no way a man as fine as Cage Harrison was single. It would only be wishful thinking on her part.

"Okay, I have shown you everything," she said making her way back to the front of *Nothing Too Old*. "How much do I owe you?" Going behind the counter she picked up her purse and took out her checkbook.

Cage leaned across the counter making her more nervous than she already was. Usually she was very confident when it came to men and knew how to flirt with them without a problem. However, Cage was throwing her. She didn't know how to act around the raw masculinity of him.

"I hate to charge you for a problem it didn't take me fifteen minutes to fix," he answered. "How about you let me take you out to dinner tonight instead so I can find out more about you?"

Jaleena knew her mouth opened and closed a couple of times before she finally had enough sense to just keep it shut. Was Cage reading her mind or something? How else would he have known she was curious about him too? Lord...he is hot with a capital H. She would be a fool to turn him down and her mama didn't raise "no" fool

"I would love to have dinner with you," she smiled shoving her checkbook back into her purse. "What time do you want to pick me up?" Jaleena was already thinking about what she was going to wear. She had a couple of new dresses in her closet that she had been saving for a special occasion. No doubt a date with the hunk in front of her would be more than special. It would be something out of this world. He just looked like he would know how to please a woman. Not that she was going to sleep with him on the first date, but one little kiss might not hurt a thing.

"I have to check and make sure I don't have any more appointments after this one. So how about I pick you up in about two hours? Unless, you want to eat earlier or later and I'll make the time for it."

"Two hours will be perfect for me. I need to get a couple of more things done around here. Here let me give you my phone number and address just in case you need to cancel." Reaching across the counter, Jaleena picked up one of her business cards and wrote her personal information on the back. She handed it to Cage and watched as he slipped it into the front pocket of his well-fitting jeans.

"Oh, I'm not about to cancel on you. I've been thinking about a way to ask you out since I walked in here. I'm going to leave, but I will see you later." Cage winked at her, picked up his bag off the floor and left, leaving her staring after him.

Chapter Eight

Jaleena didn't know how long she stood looking at the door after Cage's departure. *Was she really going out on a date with a guy she just met?* Sure, she had thought about dating a white guy before. She had never gotten the opportunity until now and Cage is sexy as hell. She wasn't about to turn him down.

God, her first crush had been on a boy named Rick Parker. His mother would have rummage sales that her mother would go to every Saturday. Of course, she would go just to see Rick. God, she had to have been around nine years old and he was about eleven.

Rick only lived in their neighborhood for about six months, but those months had been the best of her childhood. Rick and his mother were always so nice to her. They gave her a free rice krispy treat anytime they sold them. However, back then Rick was a kid and now he was a part of her past. Cage was a full grown man and here in the present. She wasn't about to miss out on this opportunity to get to know him better.

"Okay, I need to get everything closed up in here so I'll have enough time to get ready for Cage." Moving from behind the counter, Jaleena walked around her shop making sure everything was in order. She was wound up about tonight, but she couldn't leave her place of business in disarray either.

Going back to the counter, Jaleena picked up her purse and was about to leave when her cell phone rang. Digging inside, she pulled it out checked the Caller ID and rolled her eyes. Shit, she didn't have time for this right now. Yet, she knew if she let the call go to voice mail, he would just keep calling back until he got a hold of her.

Flipping the cell phone open, she asked. "What do you want? Haven't you caused me enough problems today? Are you planning to come back for a repeat performance or something?"

"Little sis, is that anyway to talk to your big brother?" Tyrell snapped back at her. "I was just calling to see if you have my money yet. You know that I'm not a patient man and I need that money from you."

Was her brother out of his mind?

She wasn't about to give him any more money especially after the way he treated her earlier. He better get that through his thick skull or he was going to be in for a rude awakening.

"I'm not giving you another penny," she tossed back. "How dare you call my phone asking for money after what you did to me? I was lucky enough Cage was able to fix your juvenile prank without too much trouble."

"Cage...are you talking about that pretty boy plumber that was there today? Why in the hell are you calling him by his first name? Never mind, I don't give a damn about his ass. I want that money and you're going to give it to me one way or another," Tyrell threatened.

Jaleena took several deep breaths and tried to calm down. Tyrell knew how to push her buttons and she wasn't going to let him get away with it tonight. She had a date she was very thrilled about. Her brother wasn't about to ruin it for her with his idle threats. If he was in some kind of trouble then he was going to have to get out of it without her help.

"Listen for the last time I'm not going to help you. You can harass me all you want, but it not going to change my mind. Goodbye, Tyrell." Jaleena abruptly disconnected the call and tossed the cell phone back into her purse. She turned off the lights and locked the door to her shop before making her way to her car and driving off.

Chapter Nine

"Did I tell you how good you smell tonight? Cage asked Jaleena as she placed the drink menu back down on the table. I noticed it when you got out of your car and meant to tell you, but I don't know if I ever did."

"No, you didn't tell me and thank you for the compliment," she said smiling at him. "I'm glad you like it. I make the soap myself. A friend of mine gave me a book a while back and I decided to try my hand at it. I'm thinking about selling it at my shop."

"Well, I can say that you should make a huge profit off it because you smell good." Cage complimented her again making her feel good.

"Thanks. I think I'm going to sell four bars for around six dollars. Who knows I might start another business adventure on the side," Jaleena grinned. She was so glad that she didn't talk herself out of this date. Cage was really good company.

Crossing her legs, Jaleena leaned toward her date and stared into Cage's gorgeous eyes. She couldn't believe how comfortable she felt around him. However, she wanted to get into his head a little more.

"I think you found out a lot about my life today because of Tyrell. So, how about you tell me more about you," she commented. "Are you an only child? Have you ever been married? Fill in the blanks for me."

Shrugging one of his wide shoulders, Cage stared at her for a moment. "There isn't much to tell. I'm the only child. When I was a kid my parents died in a plane crash, after that horrible accident, I went to live with my Uncle River. We started the plumbing business together after I graduated from college. He was the man you talked to on the phone earlier today. What else? Oh yeah, I have never been married and I don't have any kids."

"Oh, I'm so sorry to hear about your parents," Jaleena retorted. "My mother passed away several years ago and I still miss her terribly. She was my best friend in the world."

"Thank you," Cage answered. "Have you and Tyrell always had such a bad relationship?"

"Tyrell has constantly wanted his way since we were little kids. However, I think going to prison made it worse. I have tried my best to help him out, but today was the end. I'm done doing my sisterly duties when it comes to him. It's about time that he stands on his own two feet. Do you think I'm doing the right thing?"

"I don't know if you want my opinion or not," Cage hedged.

Jaleena would love to hear what Cage had to say about this. Most of her friends thought she shouldn't give up on her brother because he was family and blood needed to stick together.

"Please tell me what you think." She needed an unbiased opinion about this because she was about to go crazy trying to find ways to deal with Tyrell's self-serving ways.

"I believe in helping out your family. I wouldn't be here if my River hadn't helped me out. However, I'm not into one family member bullying another. I think you need to get Tyrell out of your life."

Finally! Someone who saw the situation in the same light as she did, she thought.

"Cage, thank you. I agree with you. I have done a lot for Tyrell and it's time for him to be a man and stand on his own. He's going to be mad as hell, but he needs this and so do I."

"Enough about our families," Cage said reaching across the table. He ran the tip of his index finger across the back of her hand. "I want to know how you are enjoying this date. I wasn't sure if you were a vegetarian or not. However, I love this steak house. The prime rib is out of this world."

Jaleena tried to pretend that Cage's touch wasn't bothering her, but it was. God, she was dying to kiss him. That full bottom lip of his was driving her crazy. Okay, she had to get her mind back on track here and keep her racing hormones in check. She wasn't some teenage girl on her first date with her crush.

"No, I eat meat. Sometimes, I don't think there's anything better in the world than a good T-bone steak with a side of hot French fries."

Winking at her, Cage ran his finger across her hand one last time before moving it. "You're my kind of woman. How about I get the waiter and we can order."

"Sounds good to me," Jaleena answered feeling relaxed and pretty good for the first time today.

While Jaleena waited for Cage to get a waiter over to their table, she went over the day's events in her head. She never dreamt when she left the house this morning that later on she would be on a date with the hunk glancing over his menu. Cage was amazing to be around. His charm was there but it was so subtle that it was almost nonexistent.

He was a far cry from the men Tyrell was shoving into her face since he got back home. Why in the world would she ever want to go out with any of the guys who landed him in prison for seven years? As far as she could tell, Cage was a good guy and she was very interested in learning more about him. She secretly hoped there would be a second date in their future.

"Are you okay?" Cage asked her making her focus on him and not her daydreams. "Your mind seemed like it was a thousand miles away."

"I'm doing perfect." Jaleena couldn't think of a better word to describe tonight. "I was just hoping that you might want a second date."

Cage was about to answer her when his cell phone rang and cut him off. He pulled it out of his jacket pocket and looked at her. "I'm sorry about this. I can let it go to voice mail."

"No, go ahead and see who it is. I don't mind at all."

Cage wished that Jaleena had told him not to answer it because he knew who it was. It was the same person who had called him five times before he left for this date tonight and he didn't want to speak with her anymore. However, he couldn't just let the phone keep ringing.

"Hello?"

"I thought you were going to call me. I have been home all day waiting to hear from you. I wanted to finish our discussion from this morning," Katlyn told him. "Did that plumbing problem turn into something bigger than you first thought?"

"Yes, it did. But I got it taken care of," he replied. He didn't want to get into this not with Jaleena sitting five feet from him. This was her time with him not Katlyn's.

"Well, you couldn't have taken a moment to call me. I need to find a way to change your mind about us. I swear that I can stop trying to make you over into what I think you should be. I would just like us to be together."

"Maybe I can come over and we can work things out like we used to." Katlyn lowered her voice on the phone trying to sound sexier, but he wasn't having any of it. She wasn't going to find a way to get back into his life.

"I apologize for not calling. I should have done that. However, I don't think the second part of your suggestion is going to happen. I meant what I said earlier. I hope you understand nothing is going to change."

Cage hated having this conversation with Jaleena right in front of him, but maybe it was for the best. Katlyn had to understand once and for all, that he wasn't coming back to her. He felt something with Jaleena and he was going to explore it as much as he could.

"Fine," Katlyn snapped and then slammed the phone down.

Shaking his head, Cage closed his phone and shoved it back into his jacket pocket. "I'm sorry again about that. I shouldn't have taken that call. I swear it won't happen again."

"Let's not worry about it," Jaleena said. "I see the waiter coming. How about we order and enjoy the rest of our date?"

"I think I love the way your mind thinks," Cage answered a second before the waiter stopped beside their table and asked for their orders.

Chapter Ten

"I had a really good time tonight," Jaleena admitted as Cage walked her back to her front door. "I can't remember the last time I had so much fun on a date just talking with a guy."

"I have to agree that you were a wonderful dinner companion. I know you said it didn't matter, but I want to apologize for taking that phone call at dinner. I shouldn't have answered it," Cage apologized as he paused on her doorstep.

"I hope it didn't give you a bad impression of me, because I would love to have a second date with you. What do you say?" Moving closer to her, Cage slid his hand behind her neck and eased her closer to his hard body.

The touch of his muscular chest against her breasts made her nipples harden instantly. Jaleena wondered how in the hell Cage could be wondering about a second date. The only thought in her mind was kissing him. Hell, she never kissed a guy on a first date, but Cage was going to be the exception to her golden rule. She had to know what his lips felt like against hers.

"Hmmm...I'm not sure if I can agree to a second date or not," she whispered sliding her arms around Cage's neck. God, she was being so forward with him, but she couldn't help it. Cage was bringing the "bad girl" out of her that she never knew existed until now.

"What do I have to do to coax a yes from those beautiful lips of yours," he asked pressing her body against his some more?

"I think a kiss might help me make a final decision." Jaleena heard the sensual sound of her voice and it even surprised her, so she could only imagine what Cage was thinking. *Was she being too forward*? At this moment, she honestly didn't care. She wanted a kiss from him and she was going to get it.

"It would be my pleasure, Gorgeous," Cage's lips brushed against hers as he spoke.

The tip of his tongue explored the side of her mouth before slipping inside. Standing on her tiptoes allowed Jaleena get the full feel of Cage's lips against hers. He moved his mouth over hers, learning its softness and taking control in a way no other man had ever done before.

The kiss was making her body come alive with passion and a burning need to have more and more, but she couldn't. Now wasn't the time to drag Cage into her bed and have her way with him. They still needed to get to know each other better, but she could tell she was going to have a hell of lot of fun doing it.

Ending the kiss, she took a couple of steps back. "We need to stop," she gasped pass her swollen lips. "I didn't know it would go this far." Her mind was reliving the hotness of their first kiss as she tried to make her traitorous body listen to her reasonable mind.

Cage moved his talented lips from her mouth, down her neck over to her ear. Pulling it between his teeth, he nibbled at it for a couple of seconds before finally releasing it. "Damn, I hate that you're right. I would love to carry you inside and make love to you for the next seventy-two hours, but I'll respect your wishes."

I'm such an idiot, Jaleena silently scolded herself as Cage moved back until their bodies were no longer touching. *I should have lived in the moment and not pushed him away.*

"I better go before I change my mind and try to seduce my way into your house." Cage sighed running his fingers through his thick brown hair. "Without a doubt, I'll be dreaming about you tonight even after I take a much needed cold shower."

Jaleena couldn't believe what Cage just told her. A part of her was blown away by his open admiration of her. While another part of her didn't know what to say back to him. How could she tell a man she just met that she was feeling a connection with him too? No, it was way too soon for these kinds of emotions. First, she had to get *Nothing Too Old* through tomorrow and then she could focus her attention on Cage.

"You sure know how to make a woman feel special," she smiled.

"Does that mean my compliment along with my kiss will get me a second date for tomorrow? I know you have the Grand Opening at your shop, but I would still love to take you out to a celebration dinner afterwards."

"Yes, I would like that," Jaleena answered immediately before she could change her mind.

An expression of satisfaction shined in Cage's eyes as he moved back towards her and pulled her into his arms. "I'll call you around six o'clock so we can finalize our plans." He gave her a soft kiss and then stepped back. Turning on his heel, he went to his car, got inside and drove off.

Standing on her porch, Jaleena went over the events of the day in her head. She was impressed with Cage's confidence. A self-assured man was such a turn-on to her. Her body was still vibrating from their kisses earlier, making her wish she hadn't let Cage leave. However, the waiting would give her more to look forward to later on.

Chapter Eleven

Flinging the phone across the room, Katlyn flung her body down on the bed as thoughts of Cage filled her mind. Why didn't he call her like he promised? Why did she have to end up calling him? He even sounded like she had bothered him with her phone call. What was wrong with him lately? He wasn't acting like the Cage she had fallen in love with.

It wasn't good for him to keep fighting his feelings for her. She already knew that he was in love with her. Why was he saying they were no longer a couple? It just didn't make any sense to her at all. She needed to take Cage on a trip so the two of them could talk about their future. She was beyond ready to be Mrs. Cage Harrison. He was the perfect man for her.

If he was worried about money he shouldn't be, because she had enough money for both of them to live off of. She could take care of them for the rest of their lives. Her husband's death left her a very wealthy woman and she wanted to share her riches with Cage.

God, she had wasted all of her youth being married to Roger McGillis. First, she had been his live in lover for several years before he finally decided to make their relationship legal. How was she supposed to know that after ten months of marriage?

He would die of a sudden heart attack leaving her everything? Sometimes things just happened in life and unfortunately Roger wasn't young enough or strong enough to keep up with her, but she wasn't going to blame herself for his death.

She did love her husband when she first married him, but after a while Roger became insulting and very mean to her. She never told anyone how he would hit her for no apparent reason. Sometimes if she didn't answer the phone quickly enough, Roger would slap her. It always came out of the blue. She was never prepared for it. All she could do was pray for the abuse to end and it finally did. No, she couldn't say that she was sad that her husband was gone and never coming back. It was past time she got some happiness back into her life and Cage was her pleasure.

Cage Harrison was the man she wanted. Katlyn knew she wasn't going to let Cage just throw her away. She would never forget the day she got up enough nerve and finally called the phone number.

Honestly, she didn't have a problem with her kitchen sink, but she had to see if all the rumors about the sexy plumber were true. Her best friend Rita Simmons had told her about Cage, but she had left out how unbelievably sexy he truly turned out to be.

She pursed him shamelessly and two weeks later they were dating each other. Shit, Cage had given her the best sex of her life. Her last husband thought he was an excellent lover, but his sexual abilities never made her see stars like Cage's love making did.

The sex between them was *so* out of this world that she offered to buy him a bigger place for his business. She didn't realize she had insulted him until, Cage had climbed out of her bed and gotten dressed. He informed her that he wasn't interested in her wealth or what it could buy for him. In addition, he had warned her if she didn't stop trying to buy him things he was going to break up with her.

Katlyn was overjoyed Cage wasn't with her because of her wealth. However, she did learn some things after the time she spent with her husband Roger. Everyone did have a price, all she had to do was find out how much Cage was worth and then he would be hers.

Of course, she wasn't about to believe that Cage had really broken up with her. He was only pissed because she offered to buy him a suit for the Mayor's Ball. She should have approached him differently about it. *How could she forget how sensitive he got was about these things?* All she had to do was find a way to get back on his good side and everything would be back the way it was.

Getting out of the bed, Katlyn picked up a cigarette off her nightstand and lit it. Taking a long puff, she blow out the smoke while thinking about a way to get herself back into Cage's life. Well, first she would have to quit smoking. Cage hated these things. So, if she wanted him in her life and bed the cigarettes would have to go.

Walking around the room, Katlyn wondered who Cage had been out with tonight. She wasn't dumb. She could tell from the way he was talking to her on the phone that he was on a date. Cage was a good-looking guy. Women were bound to be throwing themselves at him, but she couldn't let him fall for one of them. *Cage was hers!* She wasn't going to give him up, not now...not ever!

After several minutes Katlyn finally pushed Cage to the back of her mind and thought about her other problem. She was still pissed as hell at those dumb movers losing her brand new black couch. Why in the hell did she let amateurs move her furniture instead of professional movers? Now, a three thousand dollar couch was gone and she had no way of finding it. Why was she having such bad luck lately?

"Fuck that couch. I don't care if I never see it again as long as I get Cage back," Katlyn stated putting the cigarette out in the ashtray next to her bed.

Chapter Twelve

Two hours after her date with Cage, Jaleena climbed out of the cast iron Marie Louise bathtub and enjoyed the smell of her freshly made Shea Butter soap on her body. She was on her last bar so she would definitely have to make some more over the weekend.

Picking up the fluffy white towel off the sink, she wrapped it around her body as she got out of her bathtub. Her bathroom was done in all white and every time she was in here it gave her such a peaceful feeling. She left the bathroom and made her way back into her bedroom. Sitting down on the bed, Jaleena picked up the extra towel she left there. She started to dry herself off and think about the events of her day.

She still couldn't comprehend why Tyrell wanted to sabotage her new business and insult her the way he did. How dare he imply that she didn't know how to spend money correctly? He was just pissed that she hadn't wasted her money the way he had in less than six months.

If he had picked better friends over the years, instead of the kind who wanted him to waste his half of the money,

Tyrell wouldn't be in whatever mess he was in. But Tyrell loved being the center of attention as a kid and that attitude hadn't changed as they had gotten older. He was a bad seed and he would always be the trouble maker of the family.

Hell, she had even let him come and stay with her after he got out because he was her brother. All her friends kept saying *'you can't let your brother live on the street-he's family.'* So, being the nice person she was, she let Tyrell move into her extra bedroom. However, that was over now. All of his things were bagged up and sitting next to the front door. Whenever he decided to make an appearance again, his things were ready and waiting for him.

Jaleena finished drying off and put on her nightgown. She was tired and ready for bed, but she couldn't get Cage out of her mind. "I can't believe how incredible my date was with him," she said out loud. "I don't know the last time a man made me feel so special. He actually listened instead of trying to talk over me. It was about me tonight instead of his problems."

She was dying to talk to him, but it was probably too late to be calling him. Cage was probably in bed asleep like she should be, but she was too excited about tomorrow.

There was no way her body was going to let her get a good night's sleep.

If I was with Cage right now I wouldn't be thinking about sleeping either, her mind thought as she got up from the bed and turned back the covers. Without a doubt, they would find more pleasurable ways to pass the time until the early morning hours.

"Okay, I can't go down this road or I'll have to talk a cold shower. Yes, Cage does have a killer body. One that I wouldn't mind getting to know a little better," Jaleena said to herself as she crawled into bed. "However, that isn't going to happen tonight. So, I need to get my fantasies under control and get some sleep." Shoving her sexy thoughts of Cage to the back of her mind, she reached to turn out her light at the same time the phone rang.

"Hello," she answered.

"What are you wearing?" a male voice asked.

Smiling, Jaleena snuggled further into the bed and pressed the phone against her ear at the deep, sexy sound of Cage's voice. She was thrilled to be hearing from him. She decided to have a little fun with him.

"Sir, I don't know who you are. So why would I answer that question?"

"I believe you know who I am," Cage replied lowering his voice. "I was the man who hated leaving you on your doorstep. I wanted to come in and make out with you on the couch like a couple of horny college kids, but I didn't."

An erotic image of her and Cage popped into her mind and Jaleena almost choked on a moan. Shit, she hated that Cage was such a gentleman. She could tell he was a bad boy and she was dying for that side of him to come out more.

"I wouldn't have stopped you," she admitted, softly.

"Baby, you're playing with fire," Cage whispered. "Now tell me what you're wearing so I can have something to dream about tonight. You honestly have no idea how lonely I am."

"I have a pair of red cotton panties with a black star imprint above my left butt cheek. They are very cute." She wasn't really wearing that but how would he know? This was supposed to be a game of seduction.

"Are they the ones that allow your ass to peek out a little?" Cage practically moaned the words into the phone.

"Of course, I wouldn't wear anything else."

Jaleena heard the sounds of sheets being moved around, and she could only guess what Cage was doing in his big lonely bed. She already had him hot and bothered. What else could she do to make him lose control?

"Cage, are you okay? Was it something that I said?" Jaleena was hoping she was getting to him just a little.

"Baby, you shouldn't be teasing me like this. I'm going to get you back if you don't stop," Cage promised with a low rumble sending tiny shockwaves all through her body.

"Promises...promises," she sighed. "Guys have promised me things before and never come through. How can I be so sure that you will?"

"I'm not like the guys you have dated in the past. When I make a promise I keep it time and time again."

Jaleena knew she had to change the subject or she was going to be begging Cage to come over and prove her wrong. "Well...I told you what I was wearing. How about you return the favor: Boxers, briefs or nothing at all?"

"Do you really want to know? It might be too much for your young heart to handle." Cage teased.

"I'm positive that I can handle anything you want to toss my way. Now are you going to tell me or will I have to come over there and find out?" She said in a low silky voice.

Jaleena heard Cage's full masculine laugh. "Darling, I know you aren't about to come over here late as it is, so I'm going to keep what I wear to bed a surprise."

"Damn you," she tossed back then giggled. "You sure do know how to ruin a girl's night. Here I thought we were going to have a little heated phone sex."

"I love phone sex like the next man, but I can't keep you up late. I know you have a very special day tomorrow."

Jaleena was touched that Cage was thinking about her and they had only been out on one date. Tomorrow was a crucial day for her. Sleep was important, but Cage had her mind focused on things it shouldn't be on. She would never get to sleep now. She was dying to know if he slept naked.

"Can't you tell me, please," she begged.

"No, I'm going to let it simmer in the back of your mind until it drives you crazy with need. Goodnight, gorgeous," Cage whispered before hanging up on her.

"Oh, I can't believe he did that to me." Jaleena tossed the phone back on the stand next to her bed. "I swear I'm going to get him back for that," she promised as she snuggled underneath the cover and closed her eyes.

Chapter Thirteen

Standing in the back of *Nothing Too Old*, Cage watched as Jaleena interacted with her customers and saw the joy in her face. He couldn't get over how much fun he had with her last night without any sex involved. He couldn't remember the last time he didn't get laid on a first date. Katlyn was always ready to give it to him every time they went out together, but he was looking for more fulfillment than that now.

Jaleena had a fun and cute side that was so contagious. He loved how they joked around on the phone last night. He had just called her to say good night but ended up having the time of his life.

The sound of a customer calling Jaleena's name made Cage focus his attention back on the present and the woman he was falling in love with.

She was so busy that she hadn't even noticed him in the store yet. He promised to come back and being a man of his word here he was.

In all of his adult life, he had never really been in love with a woman. Sure, Katlyn was fun to hang around when they first started dating, but he never mentioned 'I love you' to her. They were more like friends with benefits and now their relationship was over. He didn't know what he had been missing until he spotted Jaleena.

She sparked a fire in him that he never knew existed until their eyes connected that day. He had wanted to jump in front of her when Tyrell was manhandling her. What kind of brother would threaten his sister for money? God, he would hate to think what would've happened to Jaleena if he had been a few minutes later. Tyrell looked pissed and ready to take out his anger on anyone in his path.

However, Tyrell wasn't about to take his frustrations out on his sister anymore. Now, that Jaleena had him in her life. He was going to make sure Tyrell understood the meaning of the word respect. *Whoa, what a minute.* What in the hell was he doing? Jaleena hadn't told him they were in a relationship. She might only want them to be friends? No! He wasn't going to stand for that. Jaleena was the woman he wanted. He would make damn sure he got his point across to her and the sooner the better.

Leaning against the back wall, Cage slid his hands into the front pocket of his jeans and watched Jaleena as she worked the room. Anyone who was watching him may have thought his relaxed pose made him seem carefree. In reality, he was plotting a way to make Jaleena a more important part of his life.

Jaleena tried to focus on counting the correct change back to the customer in front of her, but she was having a hard time. How could she concentrate on anything with Cage standing in the back of the room staring at her? She had noticed him the second he walked through the front door, but she had been too busy to say anything to him.

Double damn, how could it be possible for a man to get better looking overnight? Today, he was wearing a black T-shirt that resembled the one from yesterday. His jeans were snug in all of the right places. Just thinking about being able to strip them off his tall, muscular body made her mouth water. Lord, she had to get herself under control or she wouldn't be able to finish this final sale.

"Thank you for coming to *Nothing Too Old*. I hope you decide to come again," she said. Jaleena handed the woman the correct change and the receipt.

"I love it here," the woman replied. "It's so cute and the prices are so reasonable especially with the economy being the way it is. I'm planning to come back tomorrow and bring my sister with me. She loves a good sale."

"Thank you. I hope to see you tomorrow." Jaleena waved at the woman as she opened the door and walked outside.

A sense of pride filled Jaleena as she came around the counter and noticed several sold stickers on the big ticket items in her shop. Without a doubt, she had made over two thousand dollars today with her grand opening and things were only going to get better for her. It seems like her dream might be coming true after all.

Moving over to the door, she flipped the closed sign and locked the door. She had to do something so she wouldn't keep drooling over Cage. He had actually shown up like he promised and that meant a lot in her book. She wasn't fond of men who couldn't keep their word.

"Looks like you had a good day," a warm breath whispered by her ear.

Spinning around, Jaleena looked up into Cage's warm gray eyes and was taken aback by the wonderful scent of his cologne. "Yes, I had an excellent day. My grand opening went better than I thought it would. I'm so pleased.

Hopefully, the word will get around and more people will come tomorrow."

"Sorry, I wasn't here sooner I had a couple of jobs that ran kind of late," Cage apologized then kissed her. "Can I make it up to you?" he asked against her moist mouth. "I would hate for you to be disappointed in me."

"What do you have in mind?" Jaleena inquired running her hands over the front of Cage's shirt. She loved the hint of muscles that she felt underneath. She was counting the days until she got to see them.

"How about you finish closing up the shop and I'll be more than happy to show you?" The promise of something sexy hung in the air as Jaleena eased out of Cage's arms and took care of last minute details so she could leave.

She could only imagine what Cage had in store for her. She had never moved this fast with a man and as much as she hated to admit it; it was sort of fun living from moment to moment. Whatever Cage was thinking about doing she was more than ready for it.

Chapter Fourteen

"I can't believe how good that feels," Jaleena moaned as she leaned back on the couch. "I don't know how I made it this long without you and those magic hands."

"I'm always here to please you," Cage chuckled as his fingers moved up her calf. "Call me anytime you want this done. I'm here to please you anyway I can."

Opening her eyes, Jaleena glanced at her legs draped across Cage's hard thighs as he massaged her tired feet. It was a feeling out of this world after being on her feet for close to eight hours today. After they left *Nothing Too Old*, Cage had taken her out to dinner and then brought her back to his place surprising her with an out of this world foot massage.

"How did you know I would be so hungry?" she asked getting more comfortable on the cushions. "I never eat that much."

"I noticed how late it was when I got to your store and I knew you had to be starving. So, I wanted to treat you a nice, quiet dinner. Did you like it?" Cage asked moving his hand from her left foot over to the right one.

"Couldn't you tell how much I loved it by how quickly I gobbled everything down," she replied slightly embarrassed.

"Don't be ashamed. I love a woman that knows how to enjoy a meal. Watching you eat was turning me on," he confessed as his hand slid up her leg. "I was hoping you show that kind of passion when it comes to other things."

"What other things do you have in mind?" Jaleena asked moving her legs off Cage's hard thighs.

"Are you sure that you're ready for this?" Cage asked lifting her off the couch and straddling her body over his legs. "We haven't known each other that long. I don't want to rush you into anything."

Jaleena ran her fingers through Cage's thick brown hair and knew she didn't want to be any other place. Everything just felt so *right* when it came to him. She wanted to make love with him. He wasn't forcing her to do anything she wasn't ready for.

"I've never been more positive about anything in my life," she answered hoping that Cage lived up to her fantasy.

"God, I was hoping you would say that," Cage confessed as he stood up from the couch. "I have wanted to see this sexy body of yours naked since the first day I laid eyes on you."

"That's so good to hear," Jaleena exclaimed as she wrapped her legs around Cage's waist. "I have been dying to see your sexy ass naked too."

"Ms. Falcon, I aim to please." Walking the short distance to his bedroom, Cage tossed Jaleena down on the bed and stared into her eyes. All he could think about was making this a night she would never forget.

Chapter Fifteen

Relaxing in the middle of the bed, Jaleena watched as Cage moved away from her back over to the bedroom door. "I don't want anyone interrupting us," he said as the lock clicked loudly in the room.

"Do you get a lot of visitors?" she inquired, kicking off her shoes.

"Sometimes my Uncle River comes over to check on me and I would hate for him to walk in on us." Moving back towards her, Cage eyed her body like she was a present he was dying to unwrap and find out all of her secrets.

"When am I going to get to meet this uncle of yours? You mentioned him before, so he must be an important part of you life."

"Baby, I love my uncle," Cage said, leaning over her on the bed. "But I don't want to talk about him right now."

"Well, what would you like to do instead?"

A devilish glint came into his eyes as he stared down into hers. "I want to run my hands all over this gorgeous body of yours. Do you think you will be able to handle that? I have this wonderful scented coconut oil that I know will smell so good on your skin."

"Oh, I adore the smell of coconut oil. I use it in my hair all the time," Jaleena replied. "What do you do with it?"

Cage wasn't going to let Jaleena force him into saying the words. She knew why he had the oil and what he used it for. He bought a bottle of it the same night after his first date with her.

"How about we stop talking and get down to business?" Sitting up on the bed, Cage pulled Jaleena up so they were eye level.

"Did I tell you how much I love a man that knows how to take charge?"

Cage's left eyebrow raised a fraction at her comment before a smile pulled at his firm mouth. "I'll keep that little confession of yours in mind. However, I'm dying to feel your smooth skin beneath my hands."

Starting with the top button of her shirt, Cage slowly undid it while moving his hand slowly downward making sure that the back of his knuckles brushed her heated flesh as they went. Slipping the shirt off her shoulders, he tossed it behind him and then cupped her breasts in the palms of his hands.

The pads of his thumbs brushed over her nipples sending a pool of moisture to her panties. God, this man was too damn sexy for his own good. Even his thumbs were turning her on. *Was she some kind of kinky sex freak or something?*

"Hmmm...that feels so good," she purred in the back of her throat.

"Darling, it's only going to get better," Cage promised a second before his mouth replaced his thumbs.

Slipping her fingers through the cool strands of his hair, Jaleena succumbed to the forceful domination of his lips on her body. It was like nothing she had ever felt before: Hot, earth shattering bliss. Emotions swirled through her limbs as she fell back on the bed taking Cage with her.

Leaving her breasts he trailed a line of tantalizing kisses down her skin until he reached her belly button. He licked it a couple of times before he gave his complete attention to undoing her jeans.

He quickly got rid of them along with her underwear. "Do you know how truly beautiful you are?" Cage asked as his desire filled gaze traveled over her body.

"I'm alright," Jaleena stammered out when she finally regained her voice. She was so taken aback by the look in Cage's eyes that it left her momentarily speechless.

"I see now I have to work on you accepting a compliment," he replied before tugging his T-shirt over his head.

"SHIT! You look so hot!" The words were out of Jaleena's mouth before she could stop them.

Her eyes wandered over Cage's toned chest, down his six-pack to the noticeable bulge in the front of his jeans. There wasn't an ounce of fat on his waist. He had muscles in places that he never imagined possible.

"Thanks babe, I'm glad you like what you see." Cage worked on removing his shoes while she continued to get her fill of his perfect body.

She really must be horny if the act of Cage taking off his work boots was turning her on. She was more than ready to get to know him in every sense of the word.

The moonlight coming through the bedroom windows highlighted his body perfectly making her silently pray for Cage to touch her again. "Why are you standing there?" she whispered. "Why don't you come back over here? I'm getting lonely without you."

"Roll over on your stomach and lay perfectly still." It sounded more like a demand instead of a request. Jaleena almost thought about not doing it, but at the last minute flipped over like Cage told her.

The sound of a drawer opening behind her temporarily drew her attention making her wonder what in the world Cage was doing. She tried taking a peek over her shoulder to see what Cage was doing, but he smacked her on the ass.

Chapter Sixteen

"Ouch, that hurt," she cried out trying not to admit how much she enjoyed the little sting.

"Stop trying to sneak a peek or you'll get the same thing again," Cage warned.

"I don't believe you." Jaleena said then tried to look over her shoulder again and got another slap on her ass for her nosiness.

"Hey..." she whined.

"I told you that I would do it again. Listen to what I tell you woman, unless you like being smacked on the ass. Are you into kinky stuff?"

"No, I'm not into anything kinky," Jaleena denied, but a part of her did wonder about what sort of wild stuff Cage might be into.

"Too bad," Cage sighed behind her. "I want to show you something, but I guess now I can't." The bed dipped as he put his weight on it and a few seconds later his oil covered hands touched the middle of her back.

"Oh, your hands feel so amazing."

"Just keep still and enjoy getting pampered."

Starting high on her back, Cage moved his left hand counter clock-wise while his right hand moved clock-wise, the movement slowly started to relax the tension in her back. After a few rubs on her back, the scent of coconut oil started to fill the room and Jaleena got lost in the sensation of Cage's fingers working her body. Little by little his strokes got bigger and bigger until he was including her nape. Jaleena's body was melting under Cage's touch and she loved every second of it.

"Do you know how good this feels?" She moaned out loud. Lord, Cage was going to have her totally into him before the night was over and there wasn't going to be a thing that she could do to stop it.

"If I didn't, I do now from the sound of your moans," he breathed by her ear as his hands slipped down and massaged her butt.

"Keep on the track that you are and I can promise you that my sighs of pleasure will get louder later."

"Thanks for the information," Cage told her. "I'll try to see what I can do." His hands moved as he worked on the legs. "Do you know how sexy your legs are? I couldn't stop looking at them the day of your opening. I was imaging how they would feel wrapped around me as we made love."

"Cage Harrison, you are a bad boy. What am I supposed to say to that?"

"Have you thought about what it would be like if we made love too?"

"Oh, I have. More times than I care to admit," Jaleena confessed.

"I think it's time for you to turn over. I want to look at the front of you. I know it's just as perfect as the back."

"Are you sure about that?"

"How could anything on this beautiful body of yours be an imperfection?" Cage asked as he ran his hand down the middle of her back. "Now turn over woman so I can finish your massage."

Flipping over, Jaleena gasped when her eyes spied Cage's cock. It was at least eight inches long and thick. There was a little bit of moisture at the end and she couldn't wait until it was inside of her. Hell, he could forget all about finishing the massage and just make love to her. She reached out to touch him, but Cage brushed her hand away. "No, you can't touch me. I wouldn't be able to last if you did."

"Can I touch you later?" Jaleena asked as she dropped her hand back down on the bed.

"Babe, you can touch me all you want later, but only after I get to pleasure you." Cage's words made her warm body even hotter.

Lifting her body off the bed, he slid it towards the edge and placed her left foot in the center of his chest. With his still well oiled hands, Cage massaged the back of her calf and stopped a little bit above her knee. Usually she was really ticklish when it came to the back of her knees, but he was turning her on too much to even notice.

"Your hands should be outlawed," Jaleena panted as Cage replaced her left leg with her right on his chest. He showed her right leg the same kind of treatment.

"You know that I only do this for very special women." Cage dropped her leg and knelt between her spread thighs. She watched as he grabbed more of the oil, poured it into his hands and rubbed them together to make the liquid warm.

"How many women have been graced with your massage skills?" She asked a hint of jealousy in her voice.

He laid his hands on her thighs and slow worked the oils into her legs. Cage acted like he didn't' hear her question, but she knew that he did. It wasn't like she whispered it or anything.

"You are the first and only," he answered as his fingers came close to her wetness, but he backed away without actually touching it. "I have never thought about doing something like this until now."

"I'm glad to hear that," she confessed. "I would hate to be another notch on your massage bed."

"You will never be a notch on my anything," Cage told her as his fingers massaged the muscles in her stomach and inched their way up to her breasts. He played with her nipples before leaning over and drawing one into his wet, hot mouth.

"Shit, that feels so good," Jaleena moaned as she lifted her body off the bed. She held Cage's head to her breasts, so he would suck harder. She was so lost in the sensations that his mouth was causing that she didn't flinch when Cage thrust three of his coconut oiled covered fingers inside of her body.

The orgasm hit her so hard and fast that Jaleena thought she might pass out from it. God, she had never come with only a man's fingers before. It was something that she didn't even think was possible.

"Are you okay," Cage asked as he released her nipple and licked the side of her neck. "I didn't mean for that to happen. I wanted to be inside of you when you came for me the first time."

"You were inside of me," Jaleena giggled.

"You know that isn't what I meant," he growled taking a nip at her neck.

"Well, if you're still up to it. I'm more than ready to do it again." She couldn't wait until she felt him buried deep inside her body.

"Oh I'm willing and able." Getting off her body, she watched as Cage pulled a condom out of the drawer next to his bed and put it on. He quickly recovered her limbs with his body before she could really miss him.

Chapter Seventeen

"You are so damn beautiful," Cage whispered as he entered her with one powerful thrust. He linked their hands together and held them down on either side of her head while looking into her eyes as his body moved in and out of hers.

Jaleena got lost in his gaze while watching the way Cage's light gray eyes grew darker as she wrapped her legs around his waist. She couldn't remember ever being this close to someone before. There was something different about the way Cage loved her. It was more intense, and fulfilling.

Dropping his head, Cage's tongue slowly caressed her sensitive swollen nipples. Letting go of one of her hands, his hand burnt a path down her stomach to her leg and wrapped it more securely around his waist as his thrusts became harder and deeper.

Jaleena closed her eyes pulling at the sheets beneath her with her free hand. Lord, she was going to die from pleasure tonight and she didn't give a damn. Cage was hitting her spot in ways she wasn't sure was possible until now.

"YES!" she screamed loudly inside the room not caring she was letting herself go.

Cage let her nipple go with a loud pop. "That's it baby," he encouraged. "Tell me what you want. Let go for me. Give it to me."

"Please."

"Please, what Jaleena." Cage asked as he let go of her hand and placed it on her hips holding her in place while he had his way with her. He slowed his movements until it felt like he wasn't moving at all. "Is this what you want? Slow and easy," he whispered. "I can give it to you."

"No," Jaleena whimpered opening her eyes reconnecting her gaze with Cage's heated look. "I want it like before."

A purely masculine grin pulled at the corners of Cage's mouth as he worked his strokes harder and faster until it felt like her eyes were going to roll to the back of her head.

Jaleena's orgasm hit her out of nowhere. She screamed and clawed at Cage's back as it ricocheted through her body leaving her laying panting and her chest heaving as Cage hollered his release above her before his large body collapsed on her. She didn't know how long she laid there beneath him trying to regain control of her senses before she started squirming beneath Cage's weight.

"Cage, you're getting heavy," she complained.

"I'm sorry, sweetheart," Cage apologized as he rolled off her. He pulled her flush against his body. "I can't believe I just experienced that. It was totally..."

She knew what Cage was trying to say, but there were no words for it. She was just as blown away as he was by what just happened between them. She didn't know a man was able to bring her so close to multiple orgasms before, but Cage was about to until her body gave up.

"I know. I feel the same way," she confessed, softly more content and happy than she had been in a very long time. "How about we get some sleep and see if we can do it even better next time?"

"You think it can get better?"

"I'm a firm believer in being the best you can. What about you? Are you game, Mr. Harrison?"

"I think I'm going to like trying to be my best with you," Cage answered as he covered them with a sheet and planted a soft kiss on her mouth. "Let's get some sleep so we can get up later and see what else we can do to move up that scale."

Chapter Eighteen

Folding his arms behind his head, Cage relaxed in the middle of his rumpled bed as thoughts of Jaleena swirled around in his head. She had left over twenty minutes ago and he was still disappointed that he couldn't talk her into spending the night at his place...hell in his bed.

Most of the time he wanted a woman out of his bed soon after the love making was over, but he didn't have that reaction with her. He wanted to wake up in the middle of the night and watch her sleep. He had tried several ways to make her stay with him, but in the end she had turned him down and left. She gave him some flimsy excuse about not wanting to run late for work tomorrow, but he knew that wasn't the true reason.

Jaleena was afraid of what happened between the two of them tonight. He had never experienced such closeness with a woman before. He wasn't a virgin by far and never had claimed to be one. But Jaleena was the only woman he had ever given the option of spending the night with him and she turned him down. Hell, he *never* thought about allowing Katlyn a chance to get cozy in his bedroom for long or he wouldn't have ever found a way to get rid of her.

Removing one of his hands from behind his head, he ran it across the light covering of hair on his chest. He inhaled the wonderful scent of Jaleena that still lingered in his bed. He wondered what was next for them. He thought...no knew, they would make the perfect couple. She was the independent woman he had been searching for. It didn't hurt that she could keep up with him in bed too. That one special addition only made her *hotter* in his opinion.

Hell, he was a grown man now. Past the age of wanting a causal relationship or a roll in hay with a tight, young available body; he wanted Jaleena because she fit him and everything he desired in his life. He wasn't going to let her find a way to ease herself away from him. No, now that he had found her he wasn't about to allow Jaleena to do a vanishing act on him and what they could have.

To tell the truth he had never let the idea of being in love with someone become a conscience notion until he laid eyes on Jaleena. He wasn't saying that he wasn't like every other red blooded male in the world. Sure, in the back of his mind he had contemplated having a wife and kids. However, none of the women that he had dated or slept with made that seem like a possibility until Jaleena.

Jaleena Falcon ignited a fire within him the second she turned from arguing with her brother at *Nothing Too Old* and looked at him She had been scared and in pain, but she wasn't allowing Tyrell to see the agony she was really in at that moment. He should have run across the room and pulled him away from Jaleena. If he ever got another chance, Jaleena's brother was going to learn how to treat a woman with some respect especially someone one as unique as her.

He even gained more respect for Jaleena when she didn't flirt with him as soon as they were alone. Sometimes he would get a lot of women clients because they would gossip about him and then find odd ball reasons for him to come to their houses. Half the time nothing needed to be fixed and it would be a wasted trip on his part.

A lot of the lonely housewives in this town thought his services involved taking care of more than their plumbing problems. It was funny sometimes the excuses women would come up with to get him into their bedrooms. He would just tell them no and leave, and if they called again he would send River in his place. This usually stopped a third phone call from happening. His Godfather laughed about the numerous fake calls when it first started to occur, but after a while it got on his nerves too.

Now, when River got a hint that a plumbing call wasn't on the up and up he would go first to check it out. If it turned out to be something real, River would send him back to fix it. The new way they set up to deal with the crank calls seemed to have of stopped them for a while and he was overjoyed about it.

Jaleena wasn't the type to play games like that, but if she was, he wouldn't mind getting seduced inside of her bedroom...maybe he would find a way they could end up bathing with each other. Just the idea of being all soapy and wet in the shower had his cock leaping to life and a moan escaped from his mouth.

"God, why did I let my mind go down that road? I knew where it would lead and now Jaleena isn't here to help me with this problem."

Tossing the covers off of his aroused body, he climbed out of bed and proceeded into the bathroom. A cold shower was in his future. If Cage had his way tomorrow night, he wouldn't be taking one without help because

Jaleena's sizzling little body was going to be in there with him.

Chapter Nineteen

"I'm so glad that you came by," Jaleena whispered wrapping her arms around Cage's neck. "I thought we weren't going to see each other until later on tonight. I had this romantic dinner planned along with some other fun stuff for us to do."

"I tried to stay away, but I couldn't. I had to see you," Cage said circling his arms around her waist. "How could I stay away after the night we spent together? I was thinking maybe we should do that full body massage. I really like that. Who knows maybe next time you could give me one?"

"Hmmm...that doesn't sound too bad to me. I guess I do need to give you a special treat for helping me pass out all of those flyers about the couch. That was so sweet of you. That is a very expensive item and I know that it will bring in a lot of money if I can sell it for the listed price." "You are more than welcome," Cage said tugging her closer to his body. "I love helping out a stunning woman. I don't want a back rub, but I think that I should get something else.

"So, instead of a back rub what should I give you as a thank you?" Jaleena asked. "I though it would be something both of us enjoy."

Cage shook his head. "No, I don't think that is going to work. I want something different...something better."

"Well, do you want me to fix you a home cooked meal? I'm a pretty good cook. We could go back to my house. I could fix up something to eat instead of you taking us out to dinner and we could eat in front of the fireplace. It's sounds very sexy to me."

"Jaleena, I bet you can cook the hell out of anything your little hand touches, but that isn't what I want. I'll give you one more guess."

"God, I don't have a clue," she teased tracing Cage's bottom lip with her finger. "I thought all of my ideas were good. You might have to help me out here. Give me a hint or something. I'm sure that I'll be able to figure it out after that."

"You need a hint from me?" His tongue darted out and licked the end of her finger. "I don't know if I'm up to giving out hints or not. I know we haven't been together that long, but I think you should be able to read me by now. What do you think I *really* want from you?"

Jaleena tilted her head to the left and then to the right. She knew that Cage wanted her to kiss him, but she was having fun messing with him. She wondered how long she could keep this going on before he figured out she was teasing him.

"I got it," she grinned. "You want me to help you on your next plumbing job. I don't know anything about fixing a stopped up drain, but I can hand you all of the correct tools."

"Jaleena, stop teasing me and kiss me," Cage growled as his mouth lowered slowly towards hers.

"I thought you would never ask," she answered a second before his mouth claimed hers.

Jaleena kissed Cage back, lingering, savoring every moment of their time together. She loved how her body melted against his like they were trying to fill a hunger that neither one truly wanted fulfilled anytime soon. It was more fun working towards the end goal instead of getting it completed.

Parting her lips, she raised herself on her tiptoes so Cage could deepen the kiss. It didn't take a second coaxing from her before he eased his tongue inside of her mouth.

Without saying a word, she brushed her body against his telling Cage with body language what she wanted.

Cage swept her up into his arms and carried her from her living room into her bedroom. She didn't doubt that she was in for a very special night, because the last time she made love to Cage it left her breathless. So, there was no telling what a repeat performance was going to do to her. She was just glad she took her vitamins this morning.

Chapter Twenty

Katlyn stared at the flyer in her hand a couple of times trying to make sure she was seeing the correct thing. She had come to get her nails done and found this on the table by her favorite magazine. *Who in the hell had laid this in here?* Someone was trying to sell her black loveseat at a thrift store. What in the fuck was going on? Had those stupid drivers not really lost her property but had given it to this Jaleena Falcon woman instead?

Well, she was going to get down to the bottom of this right now. She wasn't about to be made a fool out of by anyone. She was going to get her property back and have this woman tossed in jail. Jaleena was about to find out what happened when she messed with someone who had power, money and influence.

She hadn't reported it missing, because she was too embarrassed that she let her neighbor and his friend move the furniture for a hundred dollars. However, now she was going to make sure all of them get what they had coming to them for lying to her like this.

Getting up off the couch, she stormed out of the shop with the flyer in her hand and got inside of her car. She wasn't the type of person to go inside a used furniture store, but today she was going to do it. She hated when people didn't know how to work for the things they wanted and instead took from others.

She worked hard in that hellish marriage of hers and everything she bought with her deceased husband's money was hers! She wasn't about to let anyone procure it from her. Let alone some greedy woman trying to make a quick buck off her back.

"I'm going to make sure that this woman learns her lesson about taking something that isn't hers," Katlyn said to herself as she started her vehicle and drove off towards *Nothing Too Old*.

On the drive, Katlyn let her mind travel to Cage and what happened between the two of them. *What in the hell was wrong with him?* Hasn't she been good to him since they first started sleeping with each other? She never looked down on him because he was a plumber. Most of her girlfriends told me how they tried to get him into their beds, but he turned them down. They didn't understand Cage wasn't going to crawl between the sheets with them for any price.

He actually thought he was worth something because of that run-down plumbing business of his. God, he didn't understand that he would never be in the same circle or class as the men she knew.

Sure, he made an excellent arm accessory when she needed a date. She wasn't about to deny that he could work her body like no other man ever had in her forty plus years, but that was all he would ever be worth. The T-shirt and jeans wearing Cage Harrison wouldn't know how to clean up nicely if his life depended on it. That was the one reason she was always supplying him with suits when they went out to important social events.

She couldn't have him embarrassing her by showing up dressed inappropriately. She loved doing things for Cage; however, he resented them and she never understood why. Most men would love to be schooled by an older more experienced woman. Yet, Cage fought her tooth and nail about everything.

God, he was the best lover she had ever been in bed with. Her husband liked anal sex and tried to get it every night. Most of the time she let him do it so he would just shut up and leave her alone.

However, Cage wasn't like that at all. He made her feel special each and every time they made love at her house. Only twice did she have sex with Cage in his own bed and it hurt that he made her leave, but she chalked it up to him still living with that old man, River. He constantly had excuses about not wanting him to walk in on them. Well, if he would finally put that old man in a nursing home where he belongs, she could have spent the night there more often. It would be even better if she could have gotten Cage to sell the house and move into her place.

If Cage would get over whatever was bothering him, she might be interested in making him her next husband. There was no doubt in her mind that the two of them would get along perfectly in the bedroom and it would pour out into the other aspects of their lives.

First, he would have to sell that stupid ass plumbing business of his. There would be no reason for him to work with the money she was worth. They could spend all their time together and maybe take a trip or two.

Finally arriving at her destination, Katlyn turned off her car and got out. She stood by the side of her car and looked around. She hated areas like this. They were always an unwelcome reminder of her past. The poor always had a get rich quick scheme to trick some unaware person out of their money.

Brushing her hair off her shoulders, Katlyn fixed her clothes and headed for the front door of *Nothing Too Old*. "I'm going to show this Jaleena Falcon that she doesn't mess with me or my stuff. After I finish with her, she is going to wish she had never stolen my couch."

"How dare she let him talk to me that way?"

Tyrell complained to himself inside the shady Bar and Grill. It was his favorite place to come and think. None of his friends knew about it and Jaleena sure in the hell wasn't aware of it. She would give him a lecture about being here. She would be even more pissed to know this is where he had wasted most of his money after their mother died.

He had hung out in this particular bar a lot before he got sent off to jail. Hell, everyone here was the same and no one looked down at the other person. His friends here agreed that he needed a break, but was he ever allowed to get one.

NO!

Shit, he had been struggling ever since he was a little kid. Jaleena constantly said their mother treated them fairly, but that was a damn lie. His sister always got the best of everything while he was left alone with other family members to find his own way.

So, he started stealing from other people to get what he wanted out of life. It wasn't like the people he robbed didn't have enough money to replace what he took. However, now he might have gotten in over his head. He had borrowed some money from a couple of hardcore loan sharks and he HAD to find a way to repay them or his life was going to be over. Why wouldn't Jaleena give him more money? She had it, so she should give it to him. She was his sister and that meant giving him what he needed.

Tyrell was reaching for his beer when his cell phone started ringing on the bar in front of him. Picking it up, he answered it without checking the caller ID.

"Hello."

"Tyrell, do you have the money you owe me?" The gruff voice inquired. "Your time is almost up to pay me. You do know how I'll get payment if you don't have the money."

Tyrell's body unconsciously shivered at the threat, but he kept the fear out of his voice. "Man, I told you that I don't have any money. You have to give me more time. My sister isn't giving me anything this time. I have to talk to her again."

"I'm not concerned about how you get my money as long as you get it." The phone clicked dead on the other end.

He snapped his phone closed and tossed it back on the bar. Shit, what was he going to do now? He took another sip of his drink and thought about his sister. Maybe Jaleena was right. He never wanted to do anything good with his life not even when he was a kid. He was constantly looking for the quick fix and look where it had gotten him? Nothing to even brag about or show for it, he was truly a lost cause.

Jaleena had spent her money right. She had her own business to show for it. Sure, he still thought *Nothing Too Old* was a junk yard and she was trying to relive her childhood with all of that crap, but at least it was hers.

She had been there for him so much and what did he do in return? He had tried to hurt her. He should have gone back and apologized. She might even have forgiven him and given him some extra money, but that wasn't going to happen now. That stupid plumber had to bring his ass all up in their business and now his sister wasn't even taking his phone calls. He wouldn't be able to get extra money to repay his debts. Now he had to get out of town quick and his sister's new boyfriend was to blame.

"I'm not going to let him get away with messing with my sister's mind. I'm going to find a way to make him pay and it's going to be good too." Tyrell picked up his drink. He tossed back the rest of it, placed the glass back down on the bar and then left the club.

Chapter Twenty-One

It was well past five o'clock and closing time, nevertheless Jaleena wasn't about to close with all the customers she still had inside of her shop. She couldn't believe how well those flyers had increased her business. She had only put them out yesterday, but when she got to work this morning people were standing outside waiting for her to open up.

Even the local church had come by and volunteered to help her with anything she might need assistance with. She was simply taken aback by how well everyone was getting along today. It was rather crowded and no one was acting up or causing trouble. It was refreshing to have this kind of peace. Tyrell not being here to get something started could be the reason too. It just seemed like wherever he went trouble seemed to follow. He was like a bad penny always turning up.

From the corner of her eye, she noticed a customer having a problem finding a price. She left the front of the shop and headed for the electronics section. It was usually her hot item division and she didn't want to miss out on a sale. She was halfway there when she heard someone scream.

"Where in the hell is that thief who stole my couch and is selling it in this crappy ass junk yard! I want to speak to them now!" The outraged female voice yelled.

Spinning around, Jaleena spotted a tall, elegant woman standing by the door of her store waving one of her flyers in the air. "I want an answer! Where is this person?" Everyone in the place turned and looked in her direction. She didn't know what to do. Why was this woman saying she stole her stuff? She hadn't taken anything. She had to take care of this before it got out of hand. She didn't need this woman scaring off all of her customers.

"Ma'am, I'm Jaleena Falcon. I own *Nothing Too Old*. How may I help you?" She moved towards the woman as she forgot about the customer who needed her assistance.

The woman frowned at her as she stopped circling the flyer over her head. "Excuse me...are you talking to me?"

"Yes, I heard you accuse the owner of being a thief. I'm not a thief. I didn't take anything. I hope we can get to the bottom of this problem. If you need a deal on something in here we can talk." Jaleena said pausing in front of the woman.

"Do you know who I am?" I'm Katlyn McGillis. I don't buy cheap ever. I would never want you to give me a bargain on anything you have in this dump, but I'll be more than happy to tell everyone here that you're a thief."

Jaleena took a deep breath and tried to relax her pounding heart and racing nerves. She wanted to go off on this Katlyn woman, but that wouldn't help her. She had to find out why this customer was acting this away and calmness was the only way to do it.

"What have I supposedly taken from you?"

"Do you see that black couch over there in the corner with the sticker for eight hundred dollars?"

"Yes," Jaleena answered. "I know it quite well." "It's worth three times that easily. I was told my movers had lost it, but I see now that was a lie. They gave it to you to sell in this place. I want someone to call the police so I can have her arrested for receiving stolen property." Katlyn snapped.

This couch belonged to this crazy woman in front of her. Jaleena couldn't believe her luck. She spent over a week waiting for someone to claim the couch before she decided to resell it. Now, here comes to owner causing all kinds of problems and threatening to toss her ass in jail.

"Mrs. McGillis, I'm sure we can work something out. Just give me your address and I'll have someone bring it by your house. There is no need to get the police involved."

"NO!" Katlyn yelled at her. "I want you taken to jail and I'm not going to settle for anything less than that."

Jaleena felt fear settle in her body as she got a good look at the woman's eyes. There was a lot of hate in there and she knew she wasn't going to be able to reason with her at all. She was going to get taken to jail for stealing and she hadn't done a thing. She was only selling a couch she found tossed out at the side of the road. She was so lost in thought that she didn't notice Cage coming up behind the woman in front of her until he spoke.

"Katlyn, I don't think you have to get the police involved. I'm positive that Jaleena didn't know the couch was yours," Cage said.

She watched as Katlyn whirled around so fast that she almost fell over. "Cage, what are you doing here?"

Cage hated that Jaleena was meeting his ex-girlfriend before he got a chance to tell her about Katlyn, but they had been having such a wonderful time learning about each other that he honestly hadn't wanted to ruin it by bringing her up. However, the lapse in his bad judgment was coming back to haunt him. Katlyn was here and she was about to show his girlfriend the side of her he hated.

"I'm here supporting my girlfriend. She needed me here and I'm here," he replied.

Katlyn eyed him up and down a couple of times then glanced back at Jaleena. "Is she the reason you're wearing a suit too? I could never get you to wear one for me unless I pleaded with you for a week."

"I don't have to answer you, but I will. We are going out to dinner after Jaleena closes up her shop." Cage noticed how the customers were slowly easing out the door in case something blew up. He guessed they didn't want to be witnesses to a crime.

"You never went out of your way for me like this," she complained. "I only wonder why you would do it for her." Katlyn pointed over her shoulder at Jaleena. "Was she the one you were with that time I called you around dinner time?"

Cage saw how Jaleena was listening to every word said between them. He had to get this taken care of now or Katlyn wasn't going to give up on them. "Katlyn, let me pay you for the couch. I know Jaleena wasn't trying to take anything from you. We just want to be left alone so we can move on with our relationship."

"Are you telling me you're in love with her?" Katlyn demanded. "You haven't known her that long to have developed those types of feelings."

"It doesn't take a long period of time to fall in love with someone. Sometimes you just know if you have found '*the one*'. He smiled at Jaleena and was thrilled when she smiled back at him.

"I can't believe you want to embarrass me like this. You are really offering me money for the loveseat. What if I don't want it? What if I'd rather have you instead? She can keep the damn piece of furniture!"

"Katlyn, it isn't going to make any difference. I'm not in love with you. I have never been in love with you. I told you that from the beginning. We have been over for weeks now."

"No, you're just trying to make me jealous. I'll forgive you. Let's leave and I'll treat you to dinner."

Cage hated how desperate Katlyn was acting. Her attitude wasn't going to change his mind; he wasn't going to leave with her. "Stop this and leave with some dignity."

Katlyn's eyes turned cold as she glared at him. Cage believed that his words were finally getting through to his ex-girlfriend. He only hoped that it would last this time and she wouldn't try to find a way to worm herself back into his life.

"Fine," she hissed. "I was trying to make you into something better than you are, but I see that you enjoy being on the bottom. Stay here with the other trash and see how far that gets you." Katlyn brushed past him and stormed towards the front door.

"How much do you want for the couch?" Cage yelled after her.

"Keep it. It's truly a piece of junk now after it has been in this god awful place," Katlyn hollered back before she stormed out the door and slamming it behind her.

Cage watched through the glass window of Jaleena's shop as Katlyn got into her car and drove off. She was so pissed at him that there was no telling what kind of rumors she was going to be spreading about him throughout the community, but he didn't care. He couldn't stand by and allow Katlyn to speak to Jaleena like that.

"Wow, your ex-girlfriend is something else. I don't think I have ever seen a woman that mad before," Jaleena confessed.

"I'm sorry that happened to you. Katlyn had no business storming in her like that and scaring off all of your customers. She has probably cost you a lot of money today and probably future sales."

"Oh, I'm not worrying about it. I'm pretty sure that the gossip from today will have people coming in to get a look at the woman with the "Scarlet A" across her forehead. This is a small town and something like this will be talked about for months.

"I guess I arrived in the nick of time before it got any worse," Cage said. "Katlyn can be a handful, but I want you to know that I had broken up with her before I asked you out on a date."

"I never thought you were cheating on me. You don't come across like a man who would date two women at the same time."

Moving closer to Jaleena, Cage wrapped her up in his arms. "Baby, you are the only woman I want in my life. Do you know how beautiful you truly are? You always have a smile on your face. It makes me so happy just being around you."

"Can I take you home with me?" Jaleena asked then gave him a quick kiss. "You are so good for my ego. I haven't had a man give me compliments the way you do. I think I could get used to having you around for a very long time."

"Good, I wasn't planning on going anywhere," Cage said stepping back from her.

"Thank you."

"You don't have to thank me for speaking the truth."

"No, I was thanking you for taking care of your ex-girlfriend. I thought she really was going to call the police and have me tossed in jail. In addition, she acted like the both of you were too good to be in my junk yard. I'm not quite sure if I quoted her correctly or not, but it was close enough."

"I'm sorry Katlyn hurt your feelings. You didn't deserve to be talked to like that." He reached for her again, but she swatted his hands away.

"I'm not that sensitive. I promise you I'm not going to cry. Katlyn has a right to her opinion. After dealing with my crazy brother all of these years I can handle just about anyone or anything, I'm very strong. Let me get this place closed up and we can go out to dinner my treat."

Cage watched while Jaleena moved around *Nothing Too Old* with confidence and closed everything up. He loved how proud she was of this place. Each day made him so happy that he found her and made her a part of his life. She was the perfect woman for him. He couldn't wait until he introduced her to River. He wasn't sure how well his Godfather would react to her because he was raised back in the day when the two races didn't mix.

However, he was sure that River would love Jaleena just as much as he did. He couldn't wait until he got the two of them into the same room, but for now, he had an idea of how he wanted to spend the night with his woman. Reaching inside his pants pocket, he pulled out his cell phone and turned it off before tossing it down on the counter. He didn't want any interruptions tonight from anyone.

Strolling across the room, he wrapped his arms around Jaleena's waist and planted a kiss on the back of her neck. "I was thinking about something."

"What is it?" Jaleena asked leaning back into him.

"I have wanted a new couch for a while; however, I never saw one I wanted to get until now. How about I take this one off of your hands? It would go perfectly downstairs in my basement. I can lay on it and watch all the sports that I want."

"You really want your ex-girlfriend's furniture in your house."

"It was never in Katlyn's house, but I have a suggestion how to make erase the memory," he whispered by her ear.

"What is your suggestion, Mr. Harrison?"

"Let's make it ours."

"How do you suggest we do that?"

Spinning her around, Cage picked Jaleena up in his arms and carried her over to the black couch in the center of the room. He tossed her down on it and covered her body quickly with his. "I think we should make love on it."

"I like the way your mind works," Jaleena said as she pulled his face towards hers.

"So, do I sweetheart," Cage answered before kissing his girlfriend.

Not once while they were getting lost in each other did Cage or Jaleena feel a pair of eyes watching them through the crack in the curtain in the front of the store. Dark brown eyes turned so dark that they looked onyx.

"How dare they be in there like that without a care in the world when my life is falling apart? I'm going to make both of them pay for doing this to me. I'll teach them a lesson that they will never forget."

The person peeked at them one last time before easing away from the window and blending back in with the darkness outside.

Chapter Twenty-Two

"Good Morning, sweetheart," a voice whispered before a warm kiss was planted at the side of her temple.

Opening her eyes, Jaleena gazed at Cage sitting on the bed next to her fully dressed. "Hi, yourself," she replied, softly. "How long have you been sitting there staring at me. I know I must look like something the cat dragged in." She slid up in the bed and rested her back against the headboard and then brushed her hair down with her hands.

"I have only been here for a few minutes. I love watching you sleep. You look so peaceful. I really didn't want to wake you up, but I wanted to treat you to breakfast. How does that sound?" Cage kissed her on the lips before she could move out of the way.

"God, why did you do that? I don't want to kill you with my morning breath."

"Jaleena, I love your morning breath and all don't you know that by now?"

Her heart skipped a beat at hearing Cage saying the words she had been thinking for such a while now. "I love you too."

"I kinda of thought you did, but it was good to hear." He leaned in to kiss her again, but his cell phone went off before their lips met.

"Keep that thought," Cage laughed as he held up a finger. He pulled his phone out and glanced at it. She noticed how a frown covered his handsome face.

"What is it?"

"It's the hospital," he replied. "I don't know why they would be calling me."

"Answer it." Jaleena waved at the phone in Cage's hand.

"Okay," he said. "Hello?"

Jaleena tried to hear what was going on but she couldn't make out what the other person was saying to Cage. She just noticed how the color started to drain out of his face and in her heart she knew that something was horribly wrong.

"I'll be right there," Cage uttered then hung up the phone.

"Baby, what's wrong?" She asked moving closer to Cage placing her hand on his leg. "Tell me."

"My Godfather River got shot last night. He's in serious condition. They tried calling me last night when it happened, but they couldn't get me."

"Oh my God," Jaleena uttered as she jumped out of the bed and started yanking clothes out of her closet, "Let me get dressed. I'll drive you to the hospital."
"You don't have to do that."

"Yes, I do. You aren't in any condition to drive." Jaleena tossed on some clothes and grabbed her purse. "Come on let's go." She rushed out of her bedroom door and down the hall to the front door with Cage right behind her.

The drive to the hospital seemed like it took hours instead of the usually forty-five minutes. Jaleena sent up a silent prayer of thanks that she found a parking spot near the front door. She turned in her seat and noticed the lost and haunted look in Cage's usually bright eyes.

"Honey, River is going to be okay," she promised placing her hand on top of Cage's cold one. "Go inside and I'll find you. You need a few minutes alone with River."

"Are you sure?" Cage asked as he finally looked at her. "I wanted the two of you to meet, but not like this."

"Yes, you go ahead. I'll be in right behind you." Jaleena gave Cage a gentle shove to get him moving. He couldn't go into shock now. River needed him too much.

Cage kissed her on the mouth then got out of the car rushing towards the front entrance. Jaleena watched Cage until he was out of sight. Dropping her head down on the steering wheel, she remembered how scared she was when she got the phone call about her mother. It was the worst night of her life. She prayed that Cage didn't have to go through the same thing. Sure, River wasn't his parent, but he was closest thing to it and her boyfriend loved his Godfather so much.

Doubts started to enter her mind. Was she the reason that Cage wasn't able to get here last night, because he was spending it with her at *Nothing Too Old* and back to her place? Cage turned off his phone for her and that was something he *never* did-until yesterday.

"I can't stay out here thinking about what ifs. Cage needs me in there with him and that is where I'm going." Jaleena composed herself a little more before she left the car and went in search of Cage.

Inside the hospital, she looked around the waiting room until she finally asked a nurse and she pointed her in the direction of the ICU area. Jaleena spotted Cage looking at River through a window. She could tell that he didn't know she was there yet. She eased up next to him and put her hand inside of his. Cage turned his head and looked at her. She saw the tears in his eyes.

"How is he doing?"

Looking down into the concerned upturned face of Jaleena, Cage knew he had found the woman he was meant to spend the rest of his life with. She was here with him showing true apprehension about River. It felt wonderful to have the love of a good woman. Now that he had Jaleena it was time he took care of River. He knew that River was getting too old to do this job, but he hadn't spoken up. Yet, he was going to do it now. He didn't care if River threw a fit with him. He wasn't going to let him do anymore late night jobs.

"The nurse said he's no longer in serious condition and that he had been opening his eyes off and on during the night. I'm still upset I wasn't here when they brought him in. I hate to think of him being scared and all alone. I promise that I won't do anything else to hurt or upset him. I'm going to give River anything he wants from now on."

"I believe River knows how much you care about him," Jaleena said, squeezing Cage's hand.

"If he doesn't, he will," Cage swore looking away from the window down at Jaleena.

"Cage, look," she said pointing at River. "I think he's opening his eyes."

He looked away from Jaleena and back over at River. She was right. River was opening his eyes. "I should go in there and see him. I want you to come meet him. He moved towards the door tugging Jaleena behind him."

"No, I think you need to talk to him alone. Find out what happened. I can go back to the waiting room. There will be plenty of time for us to get to know each other." She let go of his hand and stepped back. "Go and be with your Godfather."

"Are you sure?"

"Positive. It's not like I'm going anywhere."

Cage ran his hand down the side of Jaleena's face and gave her a small smile before he stepped away and rushed inside River's hospital room.

Chapter Twenty-Three

Cage blinked back tears as he sat down in the chair next to River's bed and took his hand. He grinned as River looked at him. "Old man, you almost gave me a heart attack at my young age. Do you know how bad I felt when the hospital called and told me you had gotten shot? What in the hell happened?"

"What are you crying for, boy?" River complained taking his hand back. "I'm a tough old bird. It's going to take more than a young punk trying to rob us to take me out. I almost had him until he pulled out the gun and shot me."

"Do you know who it was? Did you get a look at his face?" Cage wasn't going to stop until this person was behind bars.

"Nope, the coward was wearing a mask. I wish had seen his face," River answered. "Did the doctors tell you that if the bullet had been a little to the left I might not be able to walk."

Cage hadn't heard this news yet. He felt his stomach drop to be bottom of his shoes. "Are you going to get movement back in your legs?"

"I tried to move this early this morning when I first woke up, but I couldn't do it. It might be from the swelling in my spine. The doctor told me I might have to be in a wheelchair for a while because he doesn't want me moving too soon and injuring myself more. I'm not getting in any damn chair. I'm not that bad off."

"You will do as the doctor tells you, or I'll glue your ass to the seat if I have to! Do you understand me River?" Cage warned.

"Cage, I should never have said anything," River groaned glaring at him. "I'm not an invalid."

"I didn't say you were, but you mean the world to me. I love you and would do anything for you."

"You mean a lot to me too, son," River replied. "Enough about me are you going to tell me why they couldn't get a hold of you last night. Were you with Katlyn? I know how controlling she can be when it comes to your time. Did she have you turn off your phone?"

"No...Katlyn and I broke up a while ago," Cage answered. "We are over for good. I finally saw her for the real person she was. It was hard for her to let me go, but she finally did."

"I tried telling you about her and you acted like you weren't hearing me. At one time, you almost told me I should keep my mouth shut."

"I know and I apologize. However, enough about Katlyn I want to tell you about the new woman I'm with. She's the one I have been waiting for. I can't wait until you get to meet her. You will love her as much as I do."

"Oh, you're dating another cute little blond," River said throwing him a devilish look. "I know how much you love them. I can't wait until I get to see her. Back in the day, I was a blond man myself. There is just something about them that can get to a man don't you agree."

"What if she isn't blond?" Cage asked. He was slowly getting a sick feeling in the pit of his stomach.

"A brunette or redhead is fine too."

"River, I need to tell you something about my girlfriend Jaleena."

River frowned at him and then turned up his nose like he had a bad taste in his mouth. "Jaleena, what kind of name is that?" he asked.

"I think it's a beautiful name and it fits her perfectly."

"You aren't telling me something what it is?"

Cage closed his eyes and prayed that River wasn't going to behave the way he was thinking he would. He opened his eyes and looked directly at his Godfather.

"River, Jaleena is black. I'm in love with her and I'm going to ask her to marry me."

"Hell no," River yelled at him. "I won't let you do it. You can't let yourself get hooked up with one of them. I'd rather you be with Katlyn than a black woman."

"River, I love her and I'm going to marry Jaleena." Cage tossed back.

"I'm not going to stand for this. So, you are going to have to choose either your new girlfriend or me."

Cage didn't know what to do. How could River put him in a situation like this? He loved both River and Jaleena with everything in him. Why should he have one in his life and not the other? River had been in his life for so long that he couldn't remember a time that he wasn't.

On the other hand, Jaleena's love had given him a new lease on life. She was the polar opposite of every woman he had since he was sixteen years old. Could he really go on with the rest of his life without her in it?

He looked at River lying in the hospital bed watching him and he knew what he had to do. As much as he hated it, this had to be done and with the least amount of pain as possible.

He got up from the chair. "I'll be right back."

"Where are you going?" River asked.

"Don't worry about it. I'll be right back." Cage went through the door in search of Jaleena.

Jaleena was flipping through a book waiting for Cage to come back from seeing River when she felt someone looking at her. Glancing up, she spotted Cage standing in front of her. She tossed the book down on the chair next to her.

"How is he doing? Is he going to be okay?"

Cage's eyes ran up and down her body a couple of times before he finally answered her. "He's going to be okay, but he is going to need some extra care for the next couple of months."

"I understand and I'm here for you. I don't mind helping out where I can," she said. "Are you ready for me to meet him?"

"He's not up to any visitors right now."

Jaleena was slowly getting the feeling that Cage wasn't telling her everything. She wanted to know what was going on with him. He wasn't acting like himself at all.

"What are you keeping from me? Did he say something to you about not wanting to meet me? You know that you can tell me anything and we can work through it."

"I was telling River about you," Cage said. "He was very excited about meeting my new girlfriend until I told him that you were..."

"Black?" Jaleena filled in the word for Cage. "He doesn't want me around you or him now? Is that it?" she asked standing up.

"Yes, he told me that I had to choose between the two of you."

"You picked him over me, didn't you?" Jaleena didn't need to be told. She could tell from Cage's body language what his decision was without hearing the words.

"Jaleena, don't let this get to you. River has been through a lot in twenty-four hours. Please give him time. He'll come around and love you as much as I do." Cage reached for her, but she moved away from him. "I promise when he's back to his old self I'll make him listen about us.

Please don't get upset about this. I wouldn't be able to stand it if I hurt you."

"Cage, when you came out here to tell me these things it was over between us. You had already put the nail in your coffin. Time isn't going to change River's mind. People like him never see their views as wrong. I'll pray for him, but after he is well please don't come looking for me. In addition, I'll make sure to lose your phone number and I want you to do the same with mine."

Jaleena walked away from Cage with her head held high and not once did she look back at him. Oh, she wanted to with everything she had in her, but her willpower was stronger. She kept going until she got inside her car and that was when she finally let the tears start to fall.

Cage stood rooted to the spot where he dumped Jaleena long after she had disappeared from sight and out of the hospital's door. He still couldn't believe he had done something so stupid. *What was wrong with him?* He shouldn't let River have the kind of power over him, but he was the only family he had left and right now River needed him.

"I'm not going to lose her. I will get her back," he promised himself.

Chapter Twenty-Four

One year later

At the sound of the baby crying, Jaleena put down the roll of stickers and made her way over to the bassinet at the side of her desk. She picked up her son and patted him on the back.

"Shh....Skyler, it's going to be okay." Her baby boy calmed down instantly at the sound of her voice and touch. "Let me go and fix you a bottle. I know you're hungry. Mama's sorry that she took so long with those price tags. I'll be here sooner next time. I'm just trying to get ready for a huge sale. Don't you want us to make a lot of money?" Jaleena talked to her son like he was actually going to answer her back.

"Annie, didn't you hear Skyler crying?" She asked her new assistant as she came from the back room carrying two lamps.

"I'm sorry, Ms. Falcon," Annie apologized. "I was in the back getting these lamps out for the sale this weekend. I didn't hear him. You know I wouldn't let him cry. He was asleep when I last checked on him."

"That's okay," Jaleena said. "I think he wanted to spend some time with his mommy. You know how this little man can be sometimes. After you put those lamps down, can you finish working on that roll of stickers? I need prices on all of them. I left them on my desk out front."

"I'll get right on it," Annie said as she walked past her.

"Thank you." Jaleena smiled at Annie before she headed for the back to fix Skyler a bottle. She loved her son so much. He looks so much like his father with his gray eyes and dark brown hair. She was completely shocked to find out she was pregnant six weeks after Cage dumped her. She wanted to call him several times to tell him about the baby, but in the end she had always chickened out.

Besides her being pregnant with Cage's baby and dealing with his rejection, she got a visit from the local police. They had found out her brother Tyrell was the person who had robbed River and shot him. He was on the run and they thought she knew where he was hiding. It had taken a while before they believed she was clueless as to his whereabouts and finally left her alone. Honestly, she didn't care if she ever saw Tyrell again. He had brought too much pain into her life and it was past time that he finally stood on his own two feet.

But she did hate not having Cage in her life; she missed him way more than she was willing to admit. Honestly, she was still in love with him and it hurt that he could toss her away so easily. Since she didn't want to stay in the house and let her mind be filled with thoughts of Cage, she had gotten more involved with the local church. It helped to get her mind off of Cage a little but not a lot. He was still there late at night when she was alone in her bed.

Pushing Cage to the back of her mind for the moment, she moved around the small makeshift kitchen. Jaleena worked on getting Skyler's bottle ready while he made baby sounds against her shoulder. He was truly the most perfect gift that she could have ever wished for. Her mother would have been so in love with her grandson, spoiling him to death with way too many gifts like most proud grandparents do.

After the bottle was fixed, Jaleena was about to sit down at the table when someone called her name behind her. She spun around and found Pastor Michael there.

"Hello, Pastor Michael. What are you doing here?" She noticed that he was giving her an odd look. "Did I miss something today?"

"Jaleena, I have some bad news for you." Reaching into his pocket, he pulled out a letter. "Here let me take the baby. I can feed him while you read this."

She handed her son over to Pastor Michael and took the letter from him. "What is this?"

"Why don't you just read it?" He suggested before he took a seat at the table and gave Sklyer his bottle.

Jaleena sat down across from the Pastor and tore open the thick letter. Pulling out the sheets of paper, she embarked on reading it.

Jaleena,

I thought long and hard before I decided to write this letter to you. What can I say to you to make up for all of the horrible things I have done to you throughout the years? I just couldn't seem to be able to do anything right since I was a little kid. I always tried to blame you or mama when it was my fault. I knew when I was doing wrong and I just didn't care.

As you can tell from the outside of the envelope I'm writing this letter to you from prison. I know you won't believe this, but I do love you. I had a horrible way of showing it. I guess it's because I was so jealous of you. You constantly knew what you wanted since you were a little girl and I was searching for something with the wrong types of people.

When I heard the police were bothering you while you were pregnant I knew I had to do the right thing and turn myself in for shooting River. I needed money so bad and I thought I could get it from that plumber since you weren't about to give me anymore.

Jaleena brushed away tears as she read her brother's confession, but she didn't stop she continued.

I know you have a lot of questions and I hope that I can answer all of them with this letter. I hated Cage from the first day that I met him. I was pissed as hell that he was trying to tell me what to do and how to treat my own sister. He didn't have the right to get involved with our family business. He was a damn stranger and should have stayed in his place. I was thinking of ways to repay him. I wasn't sure how I was going to do it. I only knew I would get him.

He never knew I had been following him for a while, and saw him with that old man at his plumbing business. So, a plan began to form in my mind to get Cage back. I had to wait for the perfect opportunity and it came sooner than I thought. The last night you had your big sale, I saw you with him on that black couch and I got my opening to get him back for butting his nose in my business.

I made my way over to his plumbing business, broke in and robbed them. I was on my way out the back door when River showed up. I wasn't going to shoot the old man, but he got an attitude and tried to tackle me. I had to defend myself, so I aimed the gun at him and fired. I wasn't about to stay around and see how he was. I went around his body and out the door. I'm thrilled he didn't die or I would have gotten a longer sentence than I already have.

I'm truly sorry that I dragged you into all of this. I hope one day that you can find it in your heart to forgive me.

Your brother,

Tyrell.

Jaleena folded up the letter and placed it back in the envelope. She couldn't believe she had just read what she did. How was she supposed to handle all of this? Why was Tyrell telling her all of this now?

"How did you get this?" She asked Pastor Michael tapping the letter with her finger.

"I work at the prison with the inmates counseling them when they want to talk about the crimes they have committed. Tyrell heard you knew me and asked to see me.

He wasn't sure if you would come to see him, so he wrote the letter instead and gave it to me," Pastor Michael replied. He took the bottle out of Skyler's mouth and placed her son on his shoulder to burp him.

"My brother was right. I wouldn't have gone to see him in prison. He has done too much to me over the years. I can't let him back in my life. It wouldn't be good for either one of us."

"I'm so sorry that you're going through this. Jaleena, you seem like you have so much on your plate. Is there anything I can do for you? You know I'll be more than happy to help you out."

Jaleena picked the letter up off the table and stood up. "Do you think you can watch Skyler for a while? Annie knows how to close up the shop. She'll give you Skyler's diaper bag and I can pick him up from your house later."

"I think that will be just fine. My wife loves when we get to watch this cute little boy. She'll have him so spoiled by the time you come to get him," Pastor Michael laughed. "Do you mind me asking where you're going?"

"I just need to make some things right."

Chapter Twenty-Five

Jaleena sat inside her car staring at the building to her left. She had lost track of time, so she wasn't positive of how long she had been there. She never thought she would be here again in her life, especially after the way things ended between the two of them. Looking at the house brought back a pain she wasn't ready to deal with, but she had too because of her brother and his actions.

She really had two things to get out in the open today. Opening up her purse, she looked at the smaller envelope that held pictures of Skyler. She couldn't keep him a secret from Cage any longer. He needed to know that he was a father of a healthy, adorable baby boy.

Taking a deep breath, she brushed her hair off her face, got out of the vehicle and made her way towards Cage's house. She rang the doorbell and waited for someone to answer. It took a few minutes, but the door was finally opened. She looked down at an older man in a wheelchair and she knew this was River.

She was shocked to still see him in a wheelchair. He had gotten shot awhile ago. Cage had told her his godfather was going to be okay. Had something happened to him? Was he not going to be able to walk now? What was going on with him?

"Yes, do you need some help," River asked her "Is there a reason you're just standing there looking at me? Did you come here looking for a plumber? My partner usually doesn't take kindly to customers coming to his house instead of his place of business. However, if you leave your name and number I'll give it to Cage when he gets back from his current job."

"Sir, I don't need a plumber," Jaleena said cutting in. "I came here to apologize to you."

"Apologize about what?" River inquired.

"If you don't mind may I come in, I promise I won't take up too much of your time."

"Young lady, come in. You can have five minutes because I don't have a damn clue what you're talking about." River moved back from the door and allowed her to come inside. "Have a seat right there." He pointed to a chair about ten feet away from the door. "Tell me what this is about and then leave."

Jaleena sat down in the chair placing her purse in her lap. She was disappointed Cage wasn't here, but she guessed it meant he wasn't supposed to find out about Skyler. "Like I said I came here to apologize for what my brother did. I never knew he had such a devious side to him. If I'd had a clue he could hurt someone I wouldn't have let him do it."

"Miss, I still don't know what you are referring to," River complained. "Are you sure that you have the right place?"

"Yes sir, I have the correct place." She opened up her purse and pulled Tyrell's letter out. She didn't know the one with the pictures of Skyler fell on the floor next to her chair. "Here, please read this."

River took the envelope from her. She waited while he pulled out the letter. He had only read a few seconds before he started yelling at her. "Get the hell out of my house! How dare you show up here like this after what your brother did to me!"

Jaleena jumped up from the chair. "Sir, I'm so sorry. Please forgive me. My brother is locked up now and he won't be able to hurt anyone."

"I don't give a damn if he's locked up or not. He did this to me and I'll never forgive him or you for that matter.

Get the hell out before I call the police and put you in a cell next to him."

"Do you know that my recovery is taking longer than the doctors first thought because of my age? I might be in this chair another six months and you want me to forgive. You're out of your mind! Get out!"

"I can promise you won't see me again, sir," Jaleena said before she rushed out of the house, got into her car and raced down the street.

Chapter Twenty-Six

Cage was about six houses away from his when he saw her through his windshield, but he didn't believe his eyes. He had been dreaming about Jaleena so much that he was now seeing someone that wasn't there.

"No, it wasn't her," he said to himself as he watched the car speed off around the corner. She wouldn't come to see him not after all this time. Yet, if it was her he had to find out why she came by his house and left before he got a chance to talk to her. He didn't waste a moment leaving his car and getting inside to River. He had to find out what was going on.

"River, where are you?" Cage hollered closing the door behind him.

"I'm here," River answered coming out of the back bedroom. "What is all of the screaming about? Aren't you home a little early?"

"Who was that woman who just left here? I swear I know her."

"I don't know what you're talking about. I didn't see anyone." River looked away from him, and Cage knew River was lying to him, but why?

"River, please don't lie to me. I saw Jaleena as she was leaving this house. Tell me why she was here. I have the right to know."

"I'm not lying to you. I haven't seen or talked to anyone," River lied.

"Stop lying to me!" Cage screamed. "I gave up a lot for you after your accident. I was going to ask Jaleena to marry me, but I didn't because of your comments."

"I never asked you to give up your life for me. I only wanted you to be with a woman who was worthy of you. I just wasn't sure someone like Jaleena should be your wife. I wanted you to have the perfect family."

"Are you telling me I couldn't have the perfect family with Jaleena? What's wrong with you? I thought you loved me all these years, but I guess I was wrong. You only wanted to control me and when things weren't going your way. You blackmailed me into doing something I shouldn't have. I'm ashamed I even know you now." Cage fell down into the chair behind him and dropped his head into his hands.

"Cage, I never..." River's voice trailed off as Cage's held up his hand.

"Don't...I'm not in the mood for it. Just go. I need some peace and quiet for a few minutes."

Cage heard the sound of River's wheelchair as it moved across the hardwood floor in the direction of the kitchen. He wasn't going to allow River to take Jaleena out of his life for a second time. She came by to see him for a reason and he was going to find out what it was.

He moved to stretch his legs out in front of him when the toe of his work boot kicked something. Bending down, he picked up a small white envelope and turned it over in his hands a couple of times.

"Where did this come from?" Cage opened it up and several pictures dropped out into his hands. He flipped through them and his heart caught at the sight of the beautiful baby boy. Turning the first picture over, he saw the name Skyler Falcon on the back. However, he knew without looking at the name the baby was his.

Why hadn't Jaleena come and told him she was pregnant? Did she come to tell him about his son today and River tossed her out? Well, he wasn't going to let River control his life anymore. He was going to be a part of his son's life and if River had a problem with it so be it.

"I'm going to do everything I can to win back Jaleena's love and be a part of my son's life."

Chapter Twenty-Seven

The doorbell rang for a third time as Jaleena tried to hurry up and get to it before the person on the other side woke up Skyler. It had taken her almost an hour to get him to go to sleep. Usually he was a pretty good baby and went to sleep as soon as she put him in his crib, but tonight for some reason he was a little fussier.

"Hold on, I'm coming," she said as she opened the door and was stunned to find the man she loved on the other side. "What are you doing here?" She would never have guessed in a million years the doorbell happy intruder would be *him*.

Jaleena watched as Cage pulled something from his back pocket and held it up in front of her. It was a picture of Skyler. "May I see him? Please let me see my son...*please*."

Stepping back, she waved Cage inside the house and closed the door behind him. She couldn't let him see how excited she was to see him again after so many months of them being apart.

"I didn't realize I had lost those at your house when I went to see River," she said.

"You were there to see River? Why?"

"I had to apologize to him for what my brother did. I couldn't keep that heaviness in my heart. What Tyrell did was wrong and I wanted to try to make things right. I even showed him the letter my brother sent me, but I think that only upset him more. I had the pictures in my purse to show you. I guess they fell out when I pulled out Tyrell's letter."

"I'm glad they did or I wouldn't have ever known about Skyler," Cage said shoving the picture back into his pocket. "Can I see him now?"

"Follow me." Jaleena turned in the direction of her bedroom with Cage at her heels. She pushed opened the door and went over to the crib at the foot of her bed. "I'm redoing his nursery, so he's in here with me until I finish it.

"Cage, this is your son Skyler Falcon."

Cage looked down in the crib at his son. Tears filled his eyes as he ran an index finger down his baby smooth cheek. He had only known his son a few seconds and he was already in love with him. No, he wasn't about to lose him or Jaleena again. The two of them were his family.

"You could have told me about him," he whispered softly so he wouldn't wake up his son.

"I know and I tried several times, but I would get scared at the last minute. It was so easy for you to reject me; however, I wasn't going to let you do that my son."

"Our son," Cage corrected looking at her. "I loved you and I would have been thrilled to find out you were carrying my child. I should have been there when he was born."

"You didn't have time to take care of a pregnant ex-girlfriend and River at the same time. You had already made your choice and I made mine. We both have to deal with it now. I'm doing well, so you don't have to worry about us."

"Baby, I know that I shouldn't have let River pressure me like that. I'm so sorry. I have thought about you every day. You don't know how many times I drove past your shop and wanted to come in. I just couldn't work up the nerve because of what I had done to you. Please let me back into your life. I love you more than anything in this world. I want to watch our son grow up."

Jaleena wanted to toss Cage out on his ass and tell him never to come back, but she loved him too much. She hated being without him for these past several months. It would serve him right if she made him beg to be with her, yet she couldn't do it. She could hear the love that he had for her in his voice.

"Cage, I love you too," she confessed.

"God, Jaleena; I don't know what I would have done if you pushed me out of your life and my son's life." Cage wrapped her in his arms and yanked her to his chest. "I know this may sound crazy to you and be way too fast since we just got back together, but I'm going to do it anyway."

"Jaleena Falcon, I love you and Skyler with every fiber that I have in me. Will you end the misery I have been in for the past year and become my wife?"

"Yes, I'll marry you. Nothing will make me happier in the world."

Cage lifted her up and planted a kiss on her mouth. "I think we should celebrate our upcoming wedding, don't you?' He was about to lay her down on the bed when Skyler decided to interrupt the moment by crying his lungs out.

"I think your son has other plans. It's probably time for a diaper change. Would you like to do it?" Jaleena asked, as Cage placed her back on her feet.

"If that means I get to spend time with my son of course I want to do it. It's about time he gets used to seeing his daddy's face," Cage said as he moved away from her and picked Skyler up out of his crib.

Jaleena watched as her son stopped crying to study the new person holding him. "I think he knows who you are."

"Do you really?" Cage asked looking from Skyler to her.

"Of course, that's the reason he stopped crying. Now, let me get his stuff and I'll teach you Diaper Changing 101."

Epilogue

Two weeks later a small crowd gathered together inside the *All Faith's Church*, as they celebrated the marriage of Cage Harrison and Jaleena Falcon. The couple took their vows and then kissed, as a man in the front row held Sklyer close to his chest and sent up a silent prayer of thanks that he would be a part of this baby's life.

River didn't realize how wrong he was until Cage threatened to not allow him see his child. He never meant any disrespect to Jaleena. He was just scared when Cage almost walked out of his life. So, he made that ultimatum that he had regretted the next day but was too proud to admit to his mistake.

Luckily, he was given a second chance to prove that he could be a good Great Godfather to Sklyer and he wasn't about to blow it.

The End

Author Bio:

Marie Rochelle is a bestselling author and award winning author of interracial romances featuring black women and white men. Marie first started writing IR books about three years ago and it has been nonstop for her ever since. Her first best selling IR romance was entitled **Taken by Storm**. This bestseller will be released by Phaze later on in the year. Her hero in the book Storm Hyde won the 2006 Choice hero from REC.

In addition Ms. Rochelle has several bestselling books published through Red Rose Publishing that include: With All my Heart, Dangerous Bet; Troy's Revenge, Cover Model and Pamper Me.

Marie loves hearing from her fans. Please drop her an email at marierochelle2@yahoo.com or visit her website @ www.freewebs.com/irwriter/. She also has a discussion group fans can join and talk about her current releases. http://groups.yahoo.com/group/MarieRochelle2/. Or you can visit her website and join her regular yahoo group.

Red Rose Publishing:

Beneath the Surface- Available in ebook and print
Pamper Me- Available in ebook and print
Be With you – Available in ebook and print
Cover Model – Available in ebook and print
With all my Heart – Available in ebook and print
Love Play –
Tycoon Club Series
Dangerous Bet: Troy's Revenge: Available in ebook and print
Boss Man: Now Available-coming soon to print
Something Pumping: Coming Soon
Cole's Surrender

Special Delivery: Book 2: Heat Me Up-coming soon to print

Cobblestone Press

Special Delivery- Available Now

Phaze

All The Fixin- Available Now in both ebook and Print

My Deepest Love: Zack Available Now in both ebook and Print

Outlaw: Caught Available Now

A Taste of Love: Richard – Available Now

Loving True – Coming Soon in Sept in ebook and Print

Closer to You: Lee Coming Soon in Nov. in ebook and Print

Taken by Storm Coming Soon in Oct. in ebook and Print

The Men of CCD: Slow Seduction: Coming Soon

The Men of CCD: Tempting Turner: Coming Soon